WITCHES OF GALES HAVEN

MAGICAL
MAYHEM

LUCÍA ASHTA

MAGICAL
MAYHEM

Magical Mayhem

Witches of Gales Haven ~ Book Two

Cover design by Sanja Balan of Sanja's Covers

Editing by Ocean's Edge Editing

Proofreading by Geesey Editorial Services

For my readers,
you are the very best.
♥

"Life is meant to be lived. The more outrageously, the better."

BESSIE "NAN" GAWAMA

MAGICAL MAYHEM

CHAPTER ONE

"ARE YOU GONNA FINISH THAT?"

I jumped, squealing, my heart hammering in my chest until I discovered the source of the tiny voice. *Humphrey.* "Dammit, Humphrey, I told you not to sneak up on me like that."

"I wasn't sneaking. I can't help that I'm small and you're as distractible as my cousin Basil, and he's distracted by *everything*. He's pretty stupid."

I blinked at the small mouse as he eyed the rest of the bread on my plate. It was home-baked, and delicious of course. Now that my kids and I had officially moved into Gawama Mama House, we were enjoying Aunt Jowelle's cooking three times a day, plus snacks. It was bliss, and my waistband was stretched thanks to my regular indulgence. I'd have to go see Mo Ellen sooner rather than later for the spell that would allow me to eat all I wanted without gaining an ounce.

It'd be a dream come true, literally. I'd daydreamed about the concept of being able to down gallons of ice cream and not worry about what I was doing to my body. At forty-four, I still felt great, but let's be real, if I didn't treat my body right, I paid the price. My body was like a loan shark with a bloodied baseball bat, exacting a high cost for any transgression, with a vast arsenal of aches and pains to draw on.

My vision blurred as my eyes misted. So much good had happened since we'd returned to Gales Haven a week ago. I would have never guessed it. My family had mostly forgiven me for ditching them as my mother had. It made all the difference that I'd eventually returned when she hadn't, when she most likely never would. My aunts and nan had taken my kids under their wing, and for the first time in my children's lives I experienced the verity of the adage: *It takes a village to raise a child.*

All the weight of their well-being had been squarely on my shoulders for so long, it was a great relief to share it. Also, it was weird, really weird. I felt lighter than I had in ages.

And then there was Quade, my first love. I hadn't given a single thought to what it would be like to return to Gales Haven and find him here—and I'm only fibbing a little bit. He'd surprised me more than anyone else, the way he forgave me for running away all those years ago. I had no idea what would become of us now. I knew only that whatever spark was between us was just as combustible as it'd been nineteen years before.

Scurrying dragged my attention away from my thoughts.

"Hey! What are you doing?" I scolded.

Humphrey looked up from where he was bent over my plate, the china as old as the house, his front paws wrapped around a chunk of my delicious sourdough bread. He didn't bother to look remorseful, just smug, or as smug-looking as a mouse could get. It was his usual look.

He stared at me for a moment, then shrugged. "You can't blame me. You were staring off into the distance like you're in some kind of romance novel dreaming about your hunky man." He kept gnawing.

"How would you know a thing about romance novels?"

His head yanked back in affront. "Just because my cousin Basil is stupid..." He paused to give me a long look that suggested he was in the midst of associating me with Basil's ineptitude. "Doesn't mean I'm stupid. I read to get my exercise."

When I blinked at him again, he huffed, throwing his paws in the air in a very human gesture, dropping his bread—wait, *my* bread. "I'm little," he dragged out, eyeing me like he was waiting for me to catch up.

"Yeah, duh. I have two working eyes, ya know."

"It's the working everything else that I'm worried about."

My nostrils flared. "Hey," I snapped. Between him and Mindy the hedgehog... "Watch it, mister."

"So you get it, then?"

"Get what?"

He groaned and tossed his head back theatrically, giving me a view of the bottom of his snout, tipped in a tiny nose. "What we're talking about! Do you get how reading is exercise for a small magical creature like me?"

"Oh." I smiled. "Because you have to run along the pages to read the lines?"

"Bingo." He picked my bread back up. "So I get my exercise and learn at the same time. Those romance novels your Aunt Luanne reads sure are educational."

"I'll just bet they are."

"You'd win that bet." He chomped down on my bread, fresh from the oven this morning, dammit. "I mean, I can only learn so much about how to pleasure my woman since I have such a different body from those half-naked men on the covers."

I choked.

He ignored me.

"But I'm still picking up some great pointers. My lady friend doesn't mind a bit. In fact, she's asked me to read lots more."

I swallowed thickly. "Oh-kay. That's about enough of that."

"Fine. Can I have all this bread, then?" His little beady eyes were wide with greed.

"You don't actually think I'm going to eat it now that you've been all over it and my plate, do you?"

He shrugged those diminutive shoulders of his that were probably no more than an inch across. "Waste not, want not, my grandmama always used to say. Smart woman."

"What I need you to do is ask before you eat my food. I thought I was clear about that before."

He waved a paw at me, dismissing what I said before I even finished speaking.

"Humphrey. I mean it."

"It's *Hugh*, not Humphrey, remember? Or did you forget already?" He took another bite. "Basil can never remember what I tell him for more than a minute or two..."

"Humphrey is your given name."

"And I told you I don't like it."

I smiled evilly at him. "Don't eat my food without asking and I won't call you Humphrey, *Humphrey*."

He squinted at me. "Oh, so it's gonna be like that, is it? I thought we were friends."

"We're not friends. I only just met you a week ago, and all you do is sneak up on me, eat my food, and tell me I'm stupid."

"And...?"

"And—"

"Who are you talking to out there?" My Aunt Jowelle's voice carried through the screen door. "It's not that disgusting mouse again, is it?"

"Promise me you won't eat my food without asking," I told Humphrey, "and I won't rat you out." I chuckled. "I didn't even mean that pun."

"Yeah, that's 'cause I'm not a rat. I'm *nothing* like a rat."

"You're quite a lot like a rat, actually."

His little jaw dropped open, exposing a mouthful of bread. "Take. That. Back."

"Marla?" Aunt Jowelle was moving toward the front door.

I arched my brows at the mouse. "Promise," I mouthed.

"Take it back," he said.

"Marla Gawama?" Aunt Jowelle asked, pushing the door open.

I turned to her. "I'm here."

"I can see that plainly. So why weren't you answering me?"

"Sorry, Aunt Jowelle. I was in the middle of something."

"As long as you weren't in the middle of feeding that mouse my food."

I whipped around, but Humphrey was nowhere to be found. Sneaky devil...

"Are you finished with your breakfast?" Aunt Jowelle asked. "Nan's going to meet with the council, and she figured you might like to come along with us since you had so much to do with repairing the barrier spell."

The barrier spell protected the entire town of Gales Haven and its magical residents by powering a large dome that allowed only those who possessed magic to enter. It was the foundation of the town, established in 1803, and my daughter Macy's disruptive magic had almost broken it.

It was all fixed now.

Or, rather, it had been repaired for a fast minute until Quade's mother, Delise, hooked her magic into it.

Since Delise's magic seemed not to be further encroaching on the barrier spell, the council allowed it some time to stabilize after all that had been done to it recently. But for the last day, the council had been working with Everleigh and Kama, the most skilled of Gales Haven's spell weavers, to remove Delise's magic from where it had latched on to the original spell's threads. Everleigh, Kama, and the rest of the spell weavers they led, hadn't been having much luck. Apparently, Delise's magic, hooked soundly into the spell, was resisting their intervention. The more Delise's magic withstood them, the more cautious they became. The barrier spell was essential to the town's survival. Every risk to its integrity had to be minimized.

I looked up at Aunt Jowelle. Like me and all the Gawamas—except for my daughter Macy—she had flaming red hair, a fiery temper, and magic. "Has there been any word on Delise yet? Or Maguire?"

"No." My aunt's lips pursed in concern. "Not yet. No sign of Irma either."

Irma Lamont was one of the five council members. When it became apparent that Delise Contonn meant to weasel her way into ruling the town, Irma grabbed her and transported away. We'd expected her to return with Delise soon, but she hadn't. And Maguire, who was both Delise's husband and lapdog, had disappeared immediately after Nan told him he had to choose sides: the town or his cray-cray wife.

There hadn't been a sign of him since, and he didn't even have transporting magic like Irma did. As far as anyone knew, all he did was obey Delise's commands. But he had to have some sort of magic or he wouldn't be allowed to live in town, much less leave it on shopping trips and return again.

"What magic does Maguire have?" I asked Aunt Jowelle.

"Huh," she squeaked, and she never squeaked. "I guess I don't really know. I must've known at one point, but I don't remember."

If Maguire Contonn was one thing, he was forgettable. When he married Delise, he took her surname instead of her taking his because her family had the greater magical reputation. That set the tone for the rest of their long marriage. Maguire faded into Delise's shadow until no one considered him without her.

"I'll ask Nan to get the Registry again," I said.

"That's a good idea. Who knew you'd be so good at solving our problems?"

My heart warmed at her praise; she was stingy with it. It swept away Humphrey's comments like a wave.

The *Complete Registry of the Magical Powers and Abilities of the Residents of the Great Town of Gales Haven* was a mouthful of antiquated flourishes. It had been around since the town's founding, recording the magical abilities of every single resident. It wouldn't have forgotten Maguire.

I stood from the wicker chair I'd been lounging in while admiring the forest that surrounded Gawama Mama House. Now that Grandpa Oscar was gone, Quade used his prowess with nature to maintain it, and out here on the porch I felt connected to him. The serenity of the plants Quade coaxed into perfect health soothed me like a balm to the soul, gradually erasing all the wrongs my ex-husband had done to me—though it hadn't been entirely his fault; I was at fault too for letting him walk all over me. I should have ripped off his ding-dong when I discovered he was almost certainly cheating on me. I cringed. The imagery was disgusting. No way could I have done that.

"Marla?" Jowelle said more gently than was usually her way. My three aunts and grandmother understood that I was processing and healing. I was like a wounded animal, licking my injuries and remembering my strength.

"Are you sure you don't want us to do a treatment on you?"

I smiled gratefully at her while grabbing my plate and empty coffee cup. "It's a nice offer, but I don't want you to magically heal my heart." Really I did, but... "It's something I need to do myself."

"Well, if you change your mind, you know where to find us."

"Thanks, Aunt Jowelle. I really do appreciate it."

She patted me on the back. "Just as long as you remember now that you're home, you don't have to go it all alone. You've got us."

Tears stung the back of my eyeballs, and I swallowed a groan. My emotions were always close to the surface. If I were like this now, I didn't even want to think about what I'd be like when menopause hit. I was going to be a basket case!

Nodding silently so my voice wouldn't crack, I stepped into the house, my aunt right behind me. As soon as we entered the kitchen—her domain—she tried to take the plate from me. I held on.

She narrowed her eyes at me. "I'll wash it."

"It's okay. I'll wash it."

"You love it when you get out of cleaning."

Fact. Cleaning was the pits. There were always better things to do, like sitting around doing nothing.

"But you do all the cooking. I should clean," I said before I could regret what kind of example I was setting for the future.

She tugged at my plate. I held on, slipped out of her grip, and rushed to the sink, where I poured half a cup of detergent on the porcelain dish and began to scrub like it was my fave thing to do ever.

Aunt Jowelle tracked me like a panther, silent and menacing. Her presence settled directly behind me. "You fed that mouse from your plate again, didn't you?"

I didn't say anything, scrubbing away Humphrey's mouse cooties.

Aunt Jowelle swung around to my side, getting right up in my space.

From the dining table, my Aunt Luanne chuckled. "Breakfast and live entertainment."

"Can't ask for more than that, especially when it's Jo's cooking," Aunt Shawna added.

I didn't look their way. You're never supposed to look away from a predator when she's staring you down, right?

Jowelle whipped the plate and scrub brush out of my hand while slinging her hip into mine, butting me out of the way. "If that *mouse* ate from our heirloom china, then it's going to need more disinfecting than that. The brush too. Maybe even the sink." She peered down at the sink suspiciously, even though I hadn't put the plate down.

With a flick of her hand, the plate flew out of it to hover directly beneath the stream of water.

"That is *so* awesome," my son Clyde said from the table. "I don't think I'll ever get used to all this magic. It's amazing."

Though both my kids had been exposed to magic non-stop since our arrival in town a week ago, neither Clyde nor Macy had lost that wide-eyed awe. I hoped they never did. I preferred their wonder to their constant snark any day.

Steam began to rise off the jet of water while the cabinet beneath the sink slammed open, hitting me in the leg.

I grunted while a bottle of bleach floated out and up.

"You might want to step back." Aunt Jowelle was fierce, her attention firmly on the job at hand.

I put my hands up in surrender and backed away to the table. "Fine. Have it your way."

"My way wouldn't involve a rodent eating off of our fine china."

"You act as if I tell him to do it." I slumped into an open chair between Macy and Clyde. Everyone was at the table except for my nan. "He just does it. He doesn't ask. I've told him not to."

Clyde chuckled, tucking a crimson curl behind his ear. He needed a haircut. The curls were wilder than usual now that they were longer.

"Are you saying that a mouse is one-upping you?" he asked, snorting.

Ah, there was the teenage derision I'd so not missed...

"He's not a regular mouse, you know. He's wily, and he shows up when I'm distracted by my thoughts."

Shawna and Luanne nodded. No one said a peep when I wanted alone time, choosing to take my breakfast and other moments to myself. I'd been doing that since Devin moved out and our divorce was stamped final.

"By the way, Aunt Luanne," I added, "the mouse

reads your romance novels." I gave her a *look*, though it was unnecessary. Even Macy and Clyde had caught on to how oversexed my aunts Luanne and Shawna were. They were in their mid-to-upper sixties, but they made no attempt to conceal the fact that their sexual appetites were the size of Texas. I wanted to be like them when I grew up. I often wondered if Jowelle were to get it on as often as they did, if she'd have a one-eighty personality change.

My Aunt Luanne grinned in delight. "Really? He reads my spicy books?"

"It's how he gets his exercise, running across the pages to read each line."

"I'll have to choose my next book with that in mind, then." Her bright eyes twinkled with her signature mischief, and I knew Humphrey was in for the read of a lifetime. "Shaw, let me know if you have any suggestions."

Shawna and Luanne had been partners in crime since I was a girl. Aunt Shawna grinned as big as her sister. "I have a few ideas."

I rolled my eyes. "You two are something else."

"'Course we are," Shawna said, and the longing to be more like them tangibly pulsed through me.

"Don't go acting like you're some martyred saint, Ma," Macy chuffed.

"I'm no saint, I know that, but I do hold back more than I should," I said, wistful. How much better would life get if I didn't give a shit to the extent my two wild aunts didn't? I already didn't give much of a crap, but they didn't care what anyone thought of them—at all.

Shawna reached across the table to squeeze my hand. "It's never too late to let it all hang out, Marla love."

"That's right." Luanne nodded, her hair flying all over the place. "Once you don't care what anyone thinks of you, you're free as a bird."

"A buck naked one." Shawna beamed at me.

"Life goals." I chuckled.

"Quade ought to be able to help you let loose." Luanne gave me a big, theatrical wink, before looking at my kids as if she expected them to be amused by the prospect of their mom getting hot and heavy with her old flame.

Clyde half winced, half smiled, and Macy was suddenly fascinated by the crumbs on her plate.

Nan whisked into the kitchen with her sequined rainbow unicorn purse strapped across her chest. "What'd I miss?"

"Not much," Shawna said. "Jo's freaking out about the mouse eating Marla's food again, and Lu and I were giving Marla some advice on letting loose."

"She's too uptight," Luanne added. "She needs to let some big O's fly."

I was once more rapidly becoming desensitized to my aunts. The shock of her words hit me, but only for a moment, and it was mild.

Clyde, however, blushed furiously, while Macy pointed at him and laughed.

Nan wrapped her hands around the back of her usual seat at the kitchen table, where we ate most of our meals. "Well, at least Marla's got Quade to help with that now."

"For the last time," I said, "Quade and I aren't together. Not yet anyway."

Luanne rose from the table and sighed. "If that hunk of a man had his sights on me, I wouldn't be wasting no time."

"Yeah, well, I'm not like you, Aunt Luanne."

Luanne gave me a sad smile. "Your loss. But let me tell you, you don't gain much in life by behaving."

Shawna gathered her dish and cup and stood. "Behave at your own peril." She flicked a glance at her elder sister, who appeared consumed, watching the plate wash itself over and over amid bleach fumes. "It's easy for the days to fly by and become years of obligation when you're not having fun."

"On that note," Nan said, "let's get the kids to school before the council meeting."

"What?" Clyde startled. "You're *all* going to escort us to our new school?"

"'Course we are." Nan flattened the shiny sequins

on her unicorn. "You didn't think we'd let you go to your first day all on your own, did ya?"

Clyde sank in his chair. "No, of course not. Why would we think that?" He shot a look of pure misery to his sister, who looked as appalled at the idea as he was.

But now that we had the full support of family, I wasn't about to turn it down. By accompanying my kids to school on their first day, the Gawama women were making a clear statement: Macy and Clyde were Gawamas, through and through—no matter who their dad was. Which meant that if you messed with them, you messed with the whole Gawama clan.

Everyone in town would think twice before doing that. And I could only say that because I wasn't counting Delise.

Delise Contonn had messed with every single one of us.

What she did might have endangered the entire town of Gales Haven.

CHAPTER TWO

I SHOOK MY HEAD. "Wow. I can't believe I actually miss this place."

"You told us school is awesome here," Clyde accused.

"Compared to school in the outside world, I'm sure it is. But it's still school. High school was an awkward time for me."

"Isn't it for everyone?" Macy tucked a strand of her long, shiny dark hair behind her ear.

Clyde chuckled uncomfortably while Luanne wrapped an arm around me. "I'm surprised you had time to feel awkward, what with all the humping like rabbits you and Quade were busy doing," she said.

"Lu," I hissed. "Quade and I did *not* hump like rabbits."

That was a bit of a white lie, but Aunt Jowelle was

with us, and that severe disapproving look was firmly in place, furrowing her brow.

"I'm a light sleeper," Aunt Jowelle said, suggesting she'd heard Quade and me all those times we'd thought we were getting it on right under her nose without her knowing.

I was wondering what the hell I should say, and whether I should just own up to premarital coitus, when I noticed Macy and Clyde—Clyde as pink as a flamingo thanks to his inheriting my pale complexion—looking behind me.

Turning slowly, I came face to face with Harlow, Quade's teenage daughter. "Oh. Hi, Harlow." I forced a smile for the nice girl who was similar to Macy with her long, straight dark hair. Her eyes were all Quade though.

"I didn't notice you standing there. Um." I tugged absently on a dangling earring. "How long ago did you get here?"

She grinned. "Long enough to hear that you and Dad got down and dirty when you were my age."

"That makes you ... happy?" I asked, catching sight of Nan behind her, enjoying my comedy of errors. Nan was big on the life view of *no harm, no foul*. Unless the matter seriously threatened the well-being of the town or one of its residents, she took it all in stride.

"So happy," Harlow said. "He's been busting my

lady balls about staying out too late. Now I can tell him I know all about what he used to do when he was my age. Good luck enforcing a curfew now."

"Crap," I mumbled under my breath, scrambling for a way to fix this and coming up empty. "We didn't start having sex until our senior year, when we were almost eighteen." And by *almost*, I meant when we'd recently turned seventeen. "And you're sixteen, right?"

She flipped her hair and rolled her eyes at me, reminding me so much of Macy it was weird. Maybe it was a snarky teenage girl thing. "Obvi I'm not going to go out and start having sex just because you and my dad did. I won't have sex until I love the person and I'm ready. But this gives me all the leverage I need."

"Leverage is helpful," Aunt Luanne chimed in, being supremely unhelpful as was her way.

"Sure is." Harlow beamed and looked at Clyde and Macy. "I've been waiting for you guys. I figured you could use a friend for your first day."

Clyde stepped right up to her. "Definitely." He shot concerned glances at all us Gawama women. "They're planning on walking us in." He said it like he expected her to be as mortified by the idea as he was.

"Makes sense."

"What? Why?"

"The Gawama family name holds major clout in this town. They're reminding people that you're one of them. Kids won't mess with you overly much if they know they've got your back."

"Oh. Then I guess that's not so bad. Our last school had major bullies."

"Yeah, no bullies here. Bessie would turn their butts into stone."

"You got that right," Nan said. "I don't abide by bullying none."

Harlow smiled. "See?"

"I guess."

Macy tapped her brother on the arm. "Come on. Let's get it over with." Then she headed up the main steps to the school, looking over her shoulder until Clyde and Harlow followed.

"Wait!" I hurried after them. "Hugs."

Clyde whirled around, furiously shushing me. "Not *here*, Mom. You're embarrassing."

Catching up with them, my nan and aunts on my heels, I took my time glaring openly. "You mean, you perceive what I'm *doing* as embarrassing. You don't think I as a person am embarrassing."

While my youngest was busy not clarifying what he'd meant in the way I wanted him to, a disembodied voice called across the open space.

"Bessie Gawama, you're needed at the town hall."

It was Darnell Adams. His magic allowed him to project his voice anywhere.

Nan hitched her unicorn purse higher on her shoulder. "I've gotta go. Harlow, you'll walk them in for us and make sure everyone knows they're my great-grandchildren?"

"Sure, I'll walk them in, but everyone already knows of course. Besides, everyone's been staring at us, so I think your message has already been well received."

"Yeah," Clyde chirped. "You don't need to walk us in. Harlow will show us the way."

Macy chuckled at him and gave me a quick, discreet squeeze. "Love ya, Ma. See ya later." Then she rapidly put distance between us, flicking glances at the many students milling around us.

Nan linked her arm with mine. "Come on, Marla girl. They'll be fine. Harlow's a good kid."

The good kid smiled, saluting Nan. "I sure am. See ya!"

In seconds, Harlow and my kids climbed the remaining steps and disappeared behind the double doors of Gales Haven High School. The place looked much as it had when I'd attended the institution. Made of locally harvested wood, the complex consisted of three structures: the high school, the middle and elementary school, which was one large building, and the kindergarten. Since the school was founded along with the town, the structures were a hodgepodge framework. The first manifestation was a one-room schoolhouse as was typical for the start of the nineteenth century. As the residents multiplied, they added on to it, until it became what it is today: a one-stop shop for all things learning.

Even so, there was a limit to what the school taught, magic-wise, and every student would eventually be paired up with a mentor, who would guide the apprentice the rest of the way as their magic awakened.

Nan tugged on my arm. "Let's go. Darnell wouldn't be calling unless I was really needed."

"Right. It's just that it's my babies' first day at magic school. It has my insides all twisted in a knot."

Aunt Jowelle surged forward, setting the pace toward the parking lot and my car. "So long as you're not suggesting it's my food."

"I'd never insult your food." And I meant it. I would've sworn by the fact. Don't bite the hand that feeds you and all that—especially not when it feeds you Jowelle-quality fare.

"None of us would," Aunt Shawna added.

"Ever," Aunt Luanne echoed, and the fact that Jowelle's two fun-loving sisters would promise that was saying something.

And though Aunt Jowelle didn't turn around, her back straightened a bit more. For as stern as she was, that woman sure liked her compliments. Even her crimson hair was woven into a bun as tight as her demeanor.

"Do you think Darnell is calling because Irma's shown up with Delise?" I asked as Nan and I piled into my Subaru Forester, Jowelle in the back. Luanne rode with Shawna in her car.

"I sure hope so." Nan clicked her seatbelt on. "I've had plenty of time to think of what I want to do to that woman once I get my hands on her."

Grim curiosity sparked inside me. "What are you planning on doing?"

"I'm going to roast her over a fire pit."

"Really?" I asked, equally horrified as I was hopeful.

"Yep."

"Mom," Aunt Jowelle piped up from the back seat. "Don't freak her out with that nonsense."

"My Marla girl doesn't freak out over what I say. Do you?" Nan asked me.

I laughed. "It depends on what you say."

"Well, did the thought of me roasting that Delise and her pink poncho over fire 'freak' you out?"

"Not really ... but that's just because I can't stand the woman. And you're not actually going to do it, so it's easier to laugh."

Nan harrumphed.

I felt my eyes widen as I looked from the road up ahead to her. "You're not going to, are you?"

"She deserves it, endangering the whole town like she did. I should douse her in some of that gasoline we have stashed out back in the shed and light 'er up."

"Mom," Jowelle chided. "Don't say what you don't mean."

"Don't I mean it though?"

I honestly didn't know anymore. I'd been gone a while, and the Gawamas had personalities as fiery as they came. No one got on Nan's bad side on purpose, and definitely not Jowelle's. Not even Shawna or Luanne's. For all their fun loving and wild ways, the two younger sisters were fierce when necessary.

When I parked in front of the town hall, like a queen Nan waited for Jowelle to fetch her from the passenger seat. With one of us on either arm, she strode into the assembly hall before Luanne and Shawna caught up.

"There you are!" Stella Egerton exclaimed while she rushed forward, the shiny satin sleeves of her muumuu catching the morning light as it streamed through the large windows. Her hands were a flurry of unnecessary movement. "We received a letter from Tessa."

"Good. We could use some answers." Nan continued up the aisle, Stella walking backward as they spoke. "What about Irma and Delise? Or Maguire?"

"No news about them. But we did receive an odd complaint."

"How odd?"

"Pretty darn."

I couldn't fathom what it might be. The residents of Gales Haven embraced the bizarre and strange in the way most people from the outside world avoided it.

When Stella just kept rubbing her fingers together, waiting, Nan said, "Well? What is it?" Then she sank into the front pew.

Stella nodded sharply, her jowls wiggling slightly. "Jelly Frumpers says a leprechaun is about to cause real trouble."

"About to?" Jowelle arched her brow.

"That's what he says."

"He's predicting the future?" Nan asked pensively.

"It's what he's saying. He's also saying Marla Gawama is the one who's going to solve the case."

"Case? What case?" Jowelle asked as the doors to the hall swung open and Luanne and Shawna swept in.

As if he'd sensed Shawna's arrival, Darnell chose that moment to exit a side door and join us.

"And what's it have to do with me?" I asked the growing crowd.

"Oh." Darnell scowled, adjusting his hot pink bow tie as he walked toward us even though, as always, it was impeccable. "I'm sure it's nonsense."

"And what makes you say that?" Nan asked.

"What's going on?" Shawna asked while she and Luanne flanked me.

Darnell waved their concern away. "Jelly Frumpers says a leprechaun is in town and he's going to start causing all sorts of trouble soon."

"And that I'm supposed to solve 'the case,' whatever the hell that means," I grumbled.

"It's not like you to discount the magic of one of our residents," Nan told Darnell.

"You would have too if you'd seen him when he found me," he objected, though I'd never known Nan to discount a single thing as unbelievable. "He was drunk as a skunk off Beebee's brew. He couldn't even walk straight."

Stella nodded intently. "But he was making sense." Her arms wove in the air like she was doing the Macarena dance. "He sounded more lucid than I've ever heard him."

Darnell frowned. "He was slurring his words, Stella."

"Even so, lucid. I think a leprechaun's really going to cause problems."

"You can't be serious," I muttered mostly to myself.

"I totally am serious," she answered, oblivious to my sarcasm.

"Let me guess. If I can hear the animals, then I'll hear this leprechaun."

"Everybody will be able to hear the leprechaun," a tiny voice said from behind me, and I whirled to locate the source of it. I knew what I would find even before I spotted the hedgehog waddling adorably down a side aisle. "Leprechauns won't shut up. They think everyone wants to hear every bloody word they have to say."

"Mindy?" I asked by way of greeting.

"Who else would I be?" Then she continued muttering, "Like she knows a ton of brilliant hedge-hogs who rock the mom bod like I do."

I choked on my spit.

"What is it?" Nan asked.

"Mindy," I wheezed out as I coughed.

"Oh."

I'd told the Gawama women plenty about the tiny irreverent matriarch that only I could understand.

"And tell that Darnell man that skunks don't drink," Mindy added. "They prefer the Happy Times."

"What?" I asked. Was she really suggesting

skunks got down and toked the Gales Haven equivalent of pot?

"I *said*—"

"I heard what you said."

"Then why are you asking?"

I huffed and threw my head back. This lifetime hadn't gifted me enough patience to deal with this kind of crap.

"Do you know anything about this leprechaun situation?" I asked her instead of revealing my true feelings.

"Only that if one is indeed coming, you'd better buckle up tight. He's gonna take you on a wild ride."

Fantastic. Just what I needed. A crazy, gregarious leprechaun when I was already busy looking for Irma, Delise, and Maguire.

"Let's start with Tessa's letter," Nan said.

With a belabored sigh, I settled into the seat next to her.

CHAPTER THREE

WHEN STELLA BEGAN to read Tessa's handwritten letter, none of us interrupted. Not even Mindy uttered a peep, seeming as entranced by the outside world unfolding through Tessa's words as the rest of us. When Stella finished, Nan asked her to read the most informative portions of the three-page-long letter again.

Magic is concealed well here in Kansas, but I eventually found it, and once I did, I discovered an organized community of magic users like us, but also of all sorts of other creatures. From what I've managed to gather, there are predominant clans of vampires, werewolves, and other shapeshifters, along with those who don't shift forms but aren't human. Just yesterday I encountered a pegataur—half pegasus, half centaur—and a gnome on their travels to fulfill some important mission they were forbidden to discuss. They hailed from the Magical Creatures Academy. Yes, you read correctly. They also have schools here where they teach those with magic how to use their powers. From what I've learned so far, the afore-mentioned academy is sister to several others, among them the Magical Arts Academy, which is for witches and wizards much like us, the Magical Dragons Academy, and the Magical Objects Academy. There may be more, but these are what the traveling pegataur and gnome, both professors at the Magical Creatures Academy, shared with me.

"To think there's a school for magical creatures like me," Mindy whispered in awe. I was too absorbed by the new information to comment, though I was the only one who could hear her.

To think all this was going on when I lived in the outside world, and I'd had no idea, not even an inkling that I lived among magic users. I'd always thought Gales Haven was the only place of its kind. Now I recognized that belief for the ignorance that it was.

Like us, they hide their magic from humans because of the long history of prejudice and persecution of our kind. Apparently that hasn't changed. However, the pegataur Egan and the gnome Burl informed me that there is a dangerous movement underfoot that seeks to reveal our existence. One, the Sorcerers for Magical Supremacy, has apparently been quashed. Another, the

Voice, grows in strength as within its numbers it counts magical beings of all species. They seek to dominate humans, to wield our power to control them as they force our kind out of hiding.

Even though it was the second time Stella read this passage, she paused again while the weight of its implications settled over us. Darnell Adams, always composed, fidgeted nervously, straightening his perfectly straight bow tie. Luanne picked at her cuticles and Shawna gnawed on her lip. Jowelle frowned, the corners of her lips creasing. Nan alone remained stoically unmoved.

Stella continued after tucking her short hair behind one ear with a shaky hand: *I'd like to remain behind a bit longer to gather more information about whether this universal threat has any potential of infiltrating our safe haven. Whether or not the barrier spell is successfully repaired, I believe this to be valuable information.*

I understand that my task in leaving Gales Haven was to search for potential allies should we not manage to repair the barrier spell. At least on that front, I have definitive news. Egan and Burl introduced me to a talking pygmy owl by the name of Sir Lancelot, who is the headmaster of the Magical Creatures Academy.

"Imagine that," Mindy whispered. "An owl ... head of a school."

He has assured me that he and two sorcerers by the

names of Mordecai and Albacus, who are brothers, will find the way to aid us if necessary. He also mentioned the potential of help from a powerful intuitive witch, who dominates the elements, by the name of Clara, along with her husband, Marcelo, a highly skilled sorcerer. Sir Lancelot isn't certain what kind of help they'll be able to offer us, but he appeared confident that it would be suffi-cient to secure Gales Haven on a temporary basis. Their aid would not be a permanent measure, as they are already stretched thin with the tangible and immediate threat of exposure posed to them. The owl impressed me as highly intelligent and competent. I think we can take his word as a reasonable assessment of the situation.

Despite this possible aid, however, the only guarantee of Gales Haven's safety in the long term is to continue keeping our existence secret. I'll gather information quickly and return home so that I can help repair the barrier spell. It is our only true chance at survival.

Should you need to reach me, Sir Lancelot has provided an address—

"That's sufficient, Stella, thank you," Nan said, rubbing a gnarled hand across her cheek.

Stella folded the letter until it was an inch across. The witch was clearly nervous, unable to keep her hands still. The bright violets of her muumuu shim-mered with her continuous movements.

"It sounds bad out there," she commented. "Dangerous."

Nan slid forward on the wooden pew she occupied. "Oh, not to fret, Stella. It's a waste of energy. The barrier spell is repaired, so Gales Haven is in no immediate danger. Though Tessa's letter doesn't say specifically, it doesn't sound like anyone was aware of our community. Surely Tessa is asking for the discretion of the creatures she's discussing our community with. Knowing her, she wouldn't tell anyone any information that would lead them to finding us. That Tessa is a smart cookie."

"It's true," Darnell said, his hands back to hanging elegantly at his sides. "She's wily. She won't let on about us more than she has to. She was the right one to send as an ambassador. No matter how many publications we read about the outside world, none of them speak of magic. We needed someone on the ground to dig deeper."

Nan stood, her unicorn purse swinging around her waist. "Darnell's right. This is good news. Sure, there's danger, but there always was. That was the whole point of founding Gales Haven in the first place. To avoid it. To hide from it so we didn't have to live looking over our shoulders every damn day, waiting for the noose. Now we know more what's out there, that there are good magic users in the world that would help us."

She tucked her hands in the back pockets of her jeans, making them sag around the butt. They looked like skinny teen jeans, and they didn't fit Nan well at all. I wasn't about to tell her that. If she wanted to rock teen wear in her own way, then more power to her. I was loving her purse.

"The barrier spell is fixed from the damage Macy's magic did," she said. "So that's real good. Now, we have the Delise issue. One issue at a time, we'll get it done."

"What about the leprechaun?" Stella asked.

"We'll worry about him if he actually gets here. Jelly's track record with predictions isn't stellar."

"But this one was real. I could tell."

"Oh for toodles' sake," Darnell scoffed. "He stunk to high heaven of Beebee's brew. There's no way what he said was accurate."

Stella spun on the heel of her ballet flat, clutched the folded letter in a palm, and brought her hands to her hips. She glared. "I got a feeling about it."

"And I saw Jelly."

"Are you doubting me now? You never doubt Bessie's magical sense, why would you doubt mine?"

"Because you aren't Bessie."

Stella sucked in a breath so fast her throat whistled. She recovered quickly. "I might not be a Gawama, but I'm an Egerton. More than that, I'm an individual. My magic is as strong as yours, Darnell, so you might want to pull your head out of your ass before it gets stuck up there and I shove a cork in behind it."

A moment of silence followed Stella's colorful threat before Mindy and Shawna talked at once.

"Oh, I like her," Mindy said—while Shawna whistled and chuckled before commenting, "Stella, you've grown some brass ones."

Stella's muumuu vibrated with the intensity of her self-righteous fury as she continued to stare down Darnell. "Take it back."

He huffed, not a single hair on his silver head ruffling.

"I mean it. I can do more with my magic than create a cone of silence, you know."

"Fine." He shrugged and arched his brows like Stella was overreacting. "It looks like it's that time of the month for you."

The bodies of the women in the hall, including Mindy's, grew rigid, like we were preparing for a throwdown. The silence that followed this time was deafening. It writhed with danger like it was alive.

When the quiet drew out long enough that Darnell had the good sense to look like he'd made a mistake, Stella spoke again.

"What did you just say to me?"

"What do you mean?" Darnell laughed, but his laugh was off, as though the wizard realized how deep the shit was that he'd just landed himself in.

"I mean, do you even think before you speak?"

It would have been an odd thing to ask a man like Darnell, who was ordinarily as polished as a crystal ball. But in the circumstances it was a valid question.

"For one," Stella began, counting off on her pudgy fingers, "I don't menstruate anymore because I've already been through menopause."

Darnell's features scrunched in repulsion.

She snapped her fingers, making him jump. "Don't you dare act all grossed out by a sacred and beautiful feminine process. Menstruating is empowering, you narrow-minded man. If not for our periods, you wouldn't be here. Humanity would wither and die out without us."

"Amen, sister," Shawna called out.

"Whether we decide to use our power of reproduction is entirely up to us, and we are no lesser if we decide not to bear babes. That is our choice, and our choice alone. But don't you forget who holds the ability to bear life. Newsflash, it's definitely not you. All you do is shoot a seed out of your ding-dong that takes like half a minute, and women do all the rest."

"You tell him, Stella," Shawna heckled. "His ding-dong isn't all that."

"No, it isn't." Stella wove her neck back and forth when she said it, setting the sheet of violet satin encasing her to undulating like a wave. "His ding-dong definitely isn't all that."

"Well." Darnell ran manicured fingers across his perfectly combed hair. "This has turned unpleasant. No need to go insulting my manhood."

"And you had no right to act like you have an inkling of what it's like to be a woman."

"And you have no idea about my penis in particular."

She smiled like a wicked lizard. "Never have I been so glad not to be familiar with a male appendage."

"Your loss. I have skill you have no idea about."

"Oh-kay," Aunt Jowelle said. "I think this has gotten well out of hand."

"Indeed it has," Nan echoed, inserting herself between the two of them. "Hopefully, Darnell has learned his lesson."

"Learned a lesson? That's ridiculous. I'm a man of great experience..." He trailed off as he must have felt the laser beams shooting from every set of female eyes in the hall. "Oh, come on. You can't be serious."

Shawna pressed in on him. "Deadly," she said.

"Fine. Way to overreact."

Shawna's dark red brows nearly hit her hairline.

This was going nowhere fast, and we had better things to be worried about than Darnell Adams' chauvinism—or his ding-dong.

"Shouldn't we check the Registry about

Maguire?" I suggested. "It seems weird that no one knows anything about his magic."

Nan nodded sharply. "It's true. I asked Leonie, and not even she's ever studied his magic before, and the girl can't seem to help herself. Luanne..."

Luanne popped up from her seat, stalked past Darnell while looking down her nose at him—which required some skill since she was a foot shorter than him—and exited through the same side door he'd used. A minute later, she returned with the voluminous tome that recorded the abilities of every single resident of Gales Haven.

She plopped the book down on the table up on the dais with a dull thud and began flipping through the alphabetically organized book. "Contonn," she read out. Her eyes slowly widened as she trailed her index finger down the pages. "This can't be."

"What can't be?" I asked, rushing over to her. Everyone else, save Mindy, did the same.

"Maguire isn't listed," she said. "Neither is Delise."

"That's not possible," Darnell said. "Every resident of Gales Haven, living and dead, is listed in the Registry."

"Yeah, Mr. Smarty Pants, I know that. Delise's daddy and momma are here, as seems to be the rest of the Contonn line."

"Are Quade and Harlow there?" I asked.

"Sure are."

"But no Delise or Maguire?" I frowned. "That makes no sense at all."

Mindy waddled forward, stopping at the edge of the dais, where she struggled to climb the step. "Maybe it's the leprechaun."

I turned to face her. "Why do you think it's the leprechaun?"

"Because leprechauns get off on causing trouble."

"What's she saying?" Jowelle asked.

"She's saying it might be the leprechaun," I relayed. "But she's only saying that because she says they like to cause trouble."

"That's true," Stella said, face serious. "I've never met one, but my granny used to tell me never to mess with a leprechaun."

"And had she ever met one?" Nan asked.

"I don't think so."

"All conjecture," Darnell started. When Stella pinned him in the glare to end all glares, he shushed, glaring back at her.

"Mindy," I said, "have you ever met a leprechaun?"

"Oh yes. A leprechaun's who headbutted my George and he's never been the same since."

I gaped. Then realizing everyone was waiting for me to interpret, I deadpanned, "A leprechaun headbutted your hedgehog husband?"

She nodded.

"Well, there's no conjecture there, is there, *Darnell*?" Stella snarled.

"Come on. It's a *hedgehog*," Darnell said. "Are we going to really just take her word as proof?"

We all watched as Mindy waddled quickly backward, then charged the step, and leapt up, scrabbling to stay on the dais. She managed it. And when she started stalking Darnell, he backed away.

"She's a bit scary for something so little, isn't she?" he said, but he'd find no allies among us. He'd stuck his foot in his mouth a bit too deeply for one day.

As Mindy prowled, I got out of the way. We all did, giving her a clear shot at the man who'd sparked her ire.

"Um, I just remembered something I need to do." He rushed toward the door behind the dais and slipped through it, muttering something that sounded much like, "All women are crazy."

"I'll show him crazy when he comes out," Shawna promised, confirming I'd heard him correctly after all. The man apparently didn't know when to stop.

I didn't remember him being so narrow-minded. But then again, I was only in my twenties when I left, and I hadn't been much concerned with how Gales Haven was governed.

Mindy huffed through her little nostrils, still staring at the door that had swallowed up Darnell.

I snapped out of it first. "What about Irma? Is she still listed in the Registry?"

"Of course Irma is." Luanne flipped a couple of chunks of the book to the front. "Lamont, Lamont." She ran her fingers along pages, turning a few. "There. Lamont. Emma Lamont. Gerald Lamont. Jonathan..." She mumbled under her breath before finally looking back up, jaw slack. "There's no Irma."

Jowelle pushed between her and Shawna to grab the book. "That's not possible," she said. But though Aunt Jowelle read through all the names just as Luanne had, her conclusion was no different. She faced Nan. "Mom, what's going on?"

"I have no idea. But we'll find out."

My nan looked as determined as I'd ever seen her.

"Okay, then," I said. "So where do we start?"

No one had a good answer.

CHAPTER FOUR

NAN, Stella, Aunts Jowelle, Luanne, Shawna, and I decided that the best explanation for the Registry's absence of Delise, Maguire, *and* Irma was that they were outside of Gales Haven's borders. We all thought it unlikely that Irma would take Delise out of the town, but it seemed the only possible option. Maguire must have somehow found them and followed. Another unlikelihood.

But we were all out of guesses.

And there was one easy way to test our hypothesis.

Luanne hip-bumped Jowelle out of the way.

"Ow," Jowelle said. "So childish."

"That's right." Luanne smiled absently as she flipped through the book. "Smate..." She chewed on her lip, eating off a swath of berry purple lip gloss. "There's a Sylvia Smate and a Thomas Smate." She slammed the book shut, throwing off dust. She waved it away, pulling her head back. "No Tessa."

"So we were right," Nan said.

"It would seem like it."

"But how did Maguire find them?" I asked. "Are we to assume it's part of his magic?"

"For all we know, Delise might've put some kind of homing device on herself so he could always be at her beck and call," Shawna said.

"That would imply that Delise knew she might be taken against her will," Jowelle said. "That seems like a stretch."

"Not if she's had plans to hook into the spell for a while," I said. "She'd have to know the council wouldn't stand around and let her do it."

Nan pursed her lips. "If you hadn't realized what she was doing, it's exactly what might have happened. That Delise has been trouble since her school years. Never happy unless she was the center of attention. Willing to do whatever it took to make sure she got it. I should've seen it coming."

"Me too," Stella said. "I've always hated her and I never knew why. I should've listened to myself better."

"A lesson for all of us," Nan said, absently running her fingers along the sequins of her unicorn purse while she appeared to mull over what we should do next.

One of the double doors slammed open, hitting the wall behind it, startling us all. Mindy curled into herself until she was no larger than a tennis ball, though far pokier.

Nan's hand was over her heart. "Holy shiznickle, Jadine! You about scared me to death."

Jadine Lolly fast-walked up the aisle, her raven-black hair trailing behind her like a scarf. "Sorry, Bessie. I didn't mean to. But I need to report a crime."

"A crime?" Nan asked while Jowelle furrowed her brow. "We don't have crimes in Gales Haven. Not serious ones, anyhow. Is this a serious crime?"

Jadine was out of breath by the time she reached the dais. "Very serious," she said, and Mindy popped her head out of her ball of quills. Deciding Jadine was safe enough, she flipped over back onto her paws, not at all looking concerned about the fact that she was the only tiny creature among comparable giants.

Eyes wide, Shawna looked to Luanne, then back to Jadine. "So what is it?" she asked a bit breathlessly.

"Someone's been stealing my Spanx."

"Uh, excuse me?" I said. Surely I'd misheard her.

"Someone is stealing my Spanx."

"Oh," I said, because what else did one say to that?

"Tell us what's going on," Nan said seriously while I struggled to contain a giggle that the crazed-looking raven-haired witch would hardly appreciate. It was a good thing my kids were in school and not exposed to the full spectrum of cray-cray this town encompassed.

"I use Spanx because some things just don't tighten up the way they used to..." Jadine started.

"Hm-hmmph," Stella mumbled in understanding.

"They're damn expensive, you know, so I hand wash them. I treat them real good to make them last. I don't even hang them out on the line to dry in the sun so it doesn't wear them out. Also 'cause Jelly's my neighbor, and he likes to look over the fence at my drying line. The perv."

"Second time Jelly's come up today," Nan said. "Interesting."

Jadine narrowed her eyes at imaginary Jelly. "Did *he* take my Spanx?"

"I don't think so."

"Then why'd he come up?"

"He says a leprechaun is in town who's gonna be all sorts of trouble."

Jadine's eyes bulged. "A *leprechaun* is stealing my Spanx?"

"That's not what I said," Nan corrected.

"Well, then who's taken five pairs of Spanx from my inside drying line, hunh? Who?"

Stella turned toward me. "Jelly did say that Marla was supposed to solve whatever problems the leprechaun caused."

I couldn't help but notice how Stella's version of what Jelly said changed slightly with each time she repeated it.

"I don't think Jelly meant I was supposed to crime solve missing Spanx," I said, chuckling ... until Jadine turned her ire on me. I smiled at her awkwardly, not saying another word. I'd learned my lesson from watching Darnell Adams keep shoveling himself into a deeper hole.

"Well, somebody's gotta figure out where my Spanx went. I need them. I only have three pairs left, and that's not enough to hand wash, hang dry, and have one for each day."

"Maybe just skip the Spanx," I suggested. Wouldn't that be fast problem solving?

Jadine ran a hand along the length of her body. "And reveal what this really looks like?"

"Uh, yeah. Why not? You're a beautiful woman."

"Hell yeah I'm a beautiful woman. But I'm a curvy woman, and I like to choose which of my curves I put on display. I'm husband hunting."

I pressed my lips shut in case something tried to slip out. I wasn't going to touch that one.

Apparently none of the other Gawamas planned to either.

"Tell us the rest of the story," Nan urged. "The Spanx just disappear from the line, and that's it? Are there any clues left behind?"

"Actually, now that you ask, yeah there's some clues left behind all right. The culprit"—again she narrowed her eyes at the imagined offender—"takes *my* scissors and slices the crotch right out of my Spanx, and then he leaves the crotch pieces on my table like he's mocking me."

"How do you know it's a he?" Jowelle asked.

Jadine cocked a hip out to the side and studied her. "Are you seriously telling me you think a woman would steal a sister's Spanx and then cut the crotch out to drive her crazy? It's like he's stealing them and then mocking me about how he's not gonna use them or something. And I mean, what man would use Spanx?"

Luanne, Shawna, Nan, and I tilted our heads to the side in a maybe-some-men-use-Spanx-but-we-don't-want-to-go-there look.

"It's definitely a man," Stella affirmed, and after her heated dispute with Darnell, none of us were going to argue otherwise.

"Then this is how we're going to handle it," Nan announced, and even Mindy perked up to hear the matriarch's plan. "Stella, Jowelle, Darnell, and I will work on the Delise issue."

Stella scowled, and I wondered how long she'd hold Darnell's comments against him.

"I think it's a good idea to involve Everleigh too. The more at this point, the better."

"And us?" Shawna asked.

I wasn't sure I wanted to know what task Nan was about to assign me.

"You're with Marla. You and Lu help her figure out this mad caper."

"Mad caper?" I said. "Nan, don't you think that's a bit much...?" I stopped mid-sentence, remembering it wasn't just family here, and I wasn't supposed to question the head of the council, not in official rulings especially. "Never mind. Sorry," I added hastily.

Nan nodded her head sharply once, telling me I'd done the right thing in correcting myself. If I hadn't, she would have—and as awesome as Nan was to have as a grandmother, I doubted I would've liked what she had to say. Right now, she wasn't Nan, she was Bessie Gawama, kick-ass council foreperson whose advanced age didn't diminish her power in the least.

Nan resumed her orders. "Marla, Shawna, and Luanne, you'll investigate the crimes until they're resolved. Marla will take lead."

"Wait," I said. "Crimes?"

"Yep. I've got one of my senses about it. Jadine's Spanx is just the start."

"What about ... work?" I asked hesitantly. "My kids are settled in school now. Shouldn't I be finding a position to earn my keep?"

Nan shook her head sadly. "Marla, my girl, you've been gone from Gales Haven too long. In this town, we all step up to do what's needed. And right now, I need you to solve crimes. My magic's telling me that, and Jelly's magic is telling us that. We need you to put on your detective's hat and get to it."

I mimed putting on a hat and clicked the heels of my Converse together. "Yes, ma'am. I'm on the case of the missing Spanx. I'm about to take a bite out of crime."

No one, not even Mindy, perhaps especially not Mindy, appreciated my humor.

"This is serious," Jadine scolded me. "My Spanx are important to me."

I swallowed a monstrous groan and offered Jadine what I hoped would pass as a quasi-professional smile. "If it's important to you, it's important to me." And I even half meant it.

With a hand to her back, where I thought I could feel the slight outline of the Spanx beneath, I pointed her toward the doors. "Lead me to the scene of the crime." I swallowed a giggle, and when she spun around to look at me, I forced my face into an impassive mask.

Dang, this was going to be a challenge.

Luanne and Shawna started making their way down the aisle behind us when Nan called out, "Oh! And find Wanda. For some reason, she's a part of this too."

"I'm also coming," Mindy announced, and then I did groan. What was I, a ringmaster?

"You'd better not be dismissing my Spanx as unimportant again," Jadine threatened.

"I'm not. I was groaning at the hedgehog. She says she's coming with."

"That's good. The more help we have, the greater chance we'll have to find my missing Spanx before I run out of clean ones."

"You'll still have to buy more," I said, pointing out logic. "Unless you plan on wearing crotchless Spanx once we get them back."

"Waste not, want not. I'm not about to go buy a whole new set when all they're missing is the crotch. I've got no flabby issues going on down there."

"Oh-kay, then. Good to know." And by that I meant, *not* good to know.

Before Jadine could utter another word, I ushered her, my two sex-crazed aunts, and the tiny talking hedgehog out the double doors, wishing I could get a do-over and my return to town could actually be normal. I wouldn't be picky, just a bit ordinary would be fine. But this...?

I shook my head at my musings.

"What?" Aunt Shawna asked.

"Nothing."

"No, what?"

I sighed. "I was just thinking how crazy things have gotten and wishing for a do-over."

Luanne laughed. "Girl, we don't get do-overs in this life. You just gotta embrace the crazy and roll with it."

"She's right," Shawna said. "The sooner you start embracing the crazy, the sooner you'll start having fun."

"Well, then, bring on the fun, because crazy's already reached the station."

Luanne clapped, a clump of bracelets jingling along both arms. "That's the attitude."

"So where will we find Wanda?" I asked.

"She's probably at the shop," Shawna said.

"Which shop?"

Shawna and Luanne shared a grin, and I knew more trouble was coming.

"Why, the Cock, Coffee, and Cocoa Café of course," Shawna said, and Luanne hooted.

Of course, I thought. I wasn't even surprised anymore.

Maybe we'd find a masked criminal draped in mutilated Spanx there too.

After all, we were in Gales Haven, where the strange and bizarre happened on a daily basis. And I was on a roll.

CHAPTER FIVE

THE TOWN HALL was located prominently on Magical Main Street, occupying a sizable parcel of land, which used to be maintained by Grandpa Oscar. I assumed now that maintaining the flower gardens, grass, and trees that surrounded the hall was Quade's job.

Wanda's Cock, Coffee, and Cocoa Café was also in uptown. In a village the size of Gales Haven, nothing was that far away. Even so, our progress was painfully slow, and though I was in no great hurry to get to solving the Mad Spanx Caper—other than to get it over with—the speed of our advancement was grinding on my last nerve.

Huffing loudly, I spun to a stop, crossing my arms over my chest as I stared down at the diminutive hedgehog, thumping my foot in impatience. "Mindy.

This isn't working. You've got to let me give you a lift."

"I already told you. I don't need your help." She was out of breath from waddling as fast as she could. She wasn't a slow creature. I could tell she was moving rapidly for a hedgehog, but her legs weren't even as tall as my pinky finger. There was only so fast she could go when her stride was miniature-sized compared to ours.

I felt Jadine, Luanne, and Shawna stop behind me as I continued my attempts to persuade the most stubborn creature I might have ever met.

"I'm not saying you're some sort of useless invalid. You're just smaller than us, nothing wrong with that."

"You got that right, there's"—she had to pause to suck in breath—"nothing wrong with that."

"So now that we've got that settled, just let me give you a hand, literally. You can ride in the open palm of my hand. I won't even touch you."

"Uh," Jadine said from behind me, peering over my shoulder. "I'm pretty sure you will be touching her if she's sitting in your hand."

I rolled my eyes with abandon, free in the fact that Jadine couldn't see my face and Mindy was too focused on the path ahead to notice. Every groove in the tiled sidewalk was a potential obstacle for her.

"I *mean*, I won't be petting her or anything weird

like that. She'll be riding with her dignity intact is all I'm saying."

Mindy huffed, I didn't know if at me or if she was just trying to catch her breath. "There's nothing dignified about being carried around like I'm some baby. I'm a magical creature, you know. I'm no less important in this magical community than you are just because you're monstrously large."

"So I'm not supposed to take offense to you calling me monstrous, but you're gonna take offense to me offering you a ride so it doesn't take us one million hours to make it to Wanda's shop?"

"I didn't offer *you* a ride, did I?" she snapped. "I have better manners than that."

Groaning loudly, I went to run a hand through my hair, remembered I practically had a bird nest perched on top of my head, and dropped my hand to my side.

"Come on, Mindy. I'm not trying to fight here. I just want to get this over with so I can get on with my life."

"Oh?" Jadine piped up from behind me. "You have something more important to do than solve crimes for the town? You heard Bessie. This is your new job."

"I sure did listen to Nan, and she didn't say this was my new job."

"She kinda did, actually," Shawna added, and

when I spun to face her, she just shrugged, and added, "You know your grandmother. Once she gets her feelings about things, she's unlikely to change her mind."

Beside her, Luanne nodded. The two sisters looked so much alike with their flaming red hair, soft faces, and easy smiles. "When Mom gets one of her senses," Luanne said, "she *never* changes her mind. Like ever. Face it, Marls, you've got a brand spanking new job."

"Or should you say, brand Spanxing?" Shawna suggested, and the sisters dissolved into deep belly laughs.

Jadine narrowed her eyes at them, making her appear suddenly menacing. "Are you making fun of my Spanx right now? Because if you are..."

Her unspoken threat hung in the air. Even so, Luanne and Shawna kept right on laughing.

"We sure are," Aunt Luanne said as she caught her breath. "Surely even you can see the humor in the situation. Of all the things that could've been stolen from your house."

"Spanx," Aunt Shawna chimed in, and she and Luanne cracked up again. "We should share this one with the Gales Haven News. They'll want to know all about Marla's first mystery."

Jadine leaned toward them. "You wouldn't dare."

My crazy aunts straightened. Shawna swiped at a

tear she'd been laughing so hard. "We weren't saying it to be mean, Jadine—promise. It's just funny is all. Besides, don't you think everyone will want to know about the injustice done to you?"

"Hunh," Jadine said. "Maybe. It is pretty unjust that a woman should not only have to worry about her curves, but also worry about the Spanx she spent good money on going missing."

Luanne wrapped an arm around her shoulder, pulling Jadine toward her. "You don't have to worry about your curves. As I see it, you're just choosing to."

"I just wish I could flatten out some of them."

Shawna shrugged. "Does it really matter all that much? There's lots more to life than worrying about how we look."

"That's easy for you to say. The Gawama women are all pretty. It runs in the family. You all have amazing knockers, and you're curvy in just the right way."

I stared at Jadine. She sounded completely earnest, like she really tortured herself with comparisons between herself and other women in town.

Meanwhile, I'd never once thought myself lucky for inheriting the Gawama signature curves. For one, big boobs got in the way all the time. They made my back ache, and I had to wear industrial strength sports bras when I ran just to keep the girls from knocking me out. Growing up, and well into my twenties, I'd wished to be long and lanky. I dreamed of being willowy, probably since it was the one thing completely out of my reach. As a Gawama, willowy was an impossibility.

Aunt Luanne squeezed Jadine's shoulder and leaned into her, as if their proximity could force Jadine to take her wisdom. "I've got a few years on you." And by "a few," Luanne meant a couple of decades. "Listen to me when I tell you, you're just gonna regret it later on if you don't learn to love yourself just the way you are. It's no good to always live your life out in the future."

"She's right." Aunt Shawna was somber for once. "Trust us on this one. If you wait to be happy till you think you're perfect, you'll never be happy."

"True perfection doesn't exist, hun," Aunt Luanne added. "We're all perfectly imperfect. It's just the way it is."

Shawna squeezed her other arm. "Besides, if you really are husband hunting, you want your future man to see you confident in yourself, and you want him to like you for who you are."

"That's true," Luanne said. "Men love them a confident woman. You can take our word on that one."

Jadine was turning her face back and forth between my two sexed-up aunts as they dispensed their advice. Meanwhile Mindy had almost caught up, but not quite. It was going to be a *looooong* day.

"You two do get more men than anyone else I know," Jadine commented.

"And you know how we do it?" Luanne asked while I debated whether I could just scoop Mindy up and run with her toward Wanda's place, if only to avoid whatever my aunts were about to say.

I decided Mindy would bite me or poke me. If she didn't do that, she'd probably find another way to make my life miserable, what with her ability to place her little magical creature spies just about anywhere.

Luanne took a step away from Jadine to run her hands along her sides, emphasizing her hourglass figure and drawing the looks of a few passersby. "Shaw and I *love* our bodies. And our guys love that we love ourselves."

"And we teach them how we want to be loved," Shawna added, and I silently willed Mindy to pick up the pace, though the poor little hedgehog couldn't.

Shawna ran her hands along the length of her body just as her sister had, then swayed suggestively in her long hippie skirt. "You act like you're sex on a stick, and that's exactly how men are gonna see you. Love yourself, and they won't be able to help themselves from loving you."

"That's right," Luanne echoed.

I was pretty sure that advice was overly simplified, and not at all guaranteed to work in Jadine's case, but hey, what did I know? My aunts' love lives were never-ending sagas. Mine was a picture book, and no, not those kinds of pictures. The boring kind. *Marla likes the color red. Marla's hair is red. Marla's hair is wild.* That kind, the books you read to three-year-olds until you're ready to poke your eyeballs out you're so bored.

Jadine nodded. "Okay, okay. I can get on board with this. But I still need my Spanx. They make my caboose look amazeballs, and my booty's my best feature."

I glanced over my shoulder at them just in time to catch my aunts sharing a look, the kind that said they had lots more work to do on their current subject. Knowing them, they wouldn't let up until they convinced Jadine Lolly she was the hottest thing in all of Gales Haven—without the Spanx.

Mindy sank to her haunches at my feet and craned her neck all the way back to look at me. "I won't ride in your hand—"

"Seriously, Mindy? Are you that proud? You're an amazing hedgehog, but you're small. If you're going to help us with this case, then we can't spend all day waiting—"

"What I was about to say before you opened your

mouth"—she paused while I fought the urge to squirm under her diminutive squinty-eyed stare—"is that I'll ride on your shoulder. Like an equal."

"Fine. Great." I smiled tightly. At that point, I would've let her ride on the top of my bird's nest of hair if she'd wanted to.

Extending a hand to lift her up to my shoulder, she shouted, "What are you doing?" Though her voice was tiny, there was no mistaking her shock.

"Um." I held my hand out to her. "I'm going to help you onto my shoulder?" Wasn't that the thoughtful, efficient thing to do?

"You will do no such thing!"

"Uh, okay." I looked around, noticing the attention of my three other obligatory companions on this *mad* caper, and I was using *mad* in the *insane* sense of the word. "How are you going to get onto my shoulder then?"

By way of answering, Mindy harrumphed and began to climb. By the time she got to my shin, she was scrabbling for purchase. I was worried she'd fall and poke holes in my favorite leggings.

When she got to my knee, she had to tip upside down like a rock climber.

I realized she was going to fall a moment before she did. But I didn't manage to do anything to help her. There was no easy place to grab onto her. She was all stabby quills on the outside. Besides, she'd probably murder me in my sleep if I interfered and somehow injured her pride.

Her paws lost their grip and she fell, her tiny legs swimming aimlessly until she landed with a tinny *oomph*.

The four of us witches swept down to her level.

"Ohmygod, Mindy. Are you okay?" I asked.

When I didn't relay her reply within a total of two seconds, Luanne urged, "Well? Is she okay or not? That was a pretty nasty tumble for her."

"Mindy?" I tried again.

Mindy lay with her eyes closed and her legs in the air. She hadn't even curled into a defensive ball.

"Is she breathing?" Jadine asked.

We stared at her little underbelly, but I couldn't tell.

"Do something," Shawna told me.

"Me? What can I do?"

"You're the detective."

My life was officially insane. I was no detective!

Luanne crossed her index fingers in the air in front of her, pumping them up and down. "Do CPR or something."

"You want me to do mouth-to-mouth on a hedgehog? Please tell me you aren't serious."

From the furrowed brows, wide puppy-dog eyes, and down-turned mouths, it was apparent they were very serious.

"How would I even do that?" I pointed my lips like I was going to whistle. "Like this?" I breathed out tiny puffs of air, sure they'd see how absurd the notion was.

Shawna smiled in relief. "Good, yes! Just like that."

"I can't—"

But no one cared what I was about to say. Frantically, they pointed and gestured at Mindy, who still didn't seem to be breathing, but I wasn't sure. She was so small.

Then I remembered she had tons of kids. If I didn't save her, George would have to raise them, and George was, well … let's just say he was no Mindy.

I pushed up my sleeves, got on my knees, and leaned over her, crossing my index fingers over each other just as Luanne had. "Where's a hedgehog's heart? Do you figure it's where ours is?"

"Must be." Jadine nodded fervently, her eyes shiny as they shot from me to my patient and back again. "Just hurry."

She was right. Biting my lip, I pressed the pads of my fingers to the middle of Mindy's chest and pumped. Her chest was soft and warm, making her seem so fragile. I pumped a few times, then lowered my face to hers. "Here goes nothing," I muttered, hoping she wasn't like a dog who sniffed butts and poop.

With my lips inches from hers, her eyes popped open.

I froze as they grew impossibly wide.

"What are you doing?" she accused. "Were you about to *kiss* me?"

"Um, no. Obviously not. I was trying to save your life."

"Hmmmmhmmmm," she said in a way that told me she didn't believe me one bit.

"Seriously. You weren't breathing."

Aunt Luanne, Aunt Shawna, and Jadine nodded.

"You really weren't," Aunt Shawna said.

"'Course I was," Mindy said, before adding to me, "Do you mind?"

I backed right the hell up.

Mindy cycled her legs a few times, then popped right-side up. "Hold out your arm."

I did.

"No, not like that. Lean it against your knee."

When I positioned my body to her satisfaction, she resumed her climb. I didn't dare move, even as she trash talked all the way up to my shoulder.

"See," she said like she hadn't almost died. "All you needed to do was kneel for me. Why didn't you think of that? You're supposed to be the smart detective here."

I rolled my eyes so hard my eyeballs ached from the effort, but I didn't respond. What would be the point? The tiny dictator believed what she wanted to believe.

When she reached my shoulder, she dug her tiny claws in until I could feel them through my sweater. She was definitely going to snag it.

"Well?" she announced. "What are you waiting for? I thought you were in some big hurry."

Wondering how long it would take for the mini creature to drive me fully crazy, I set off toward Wanda's.

"I can't wait to tell George how you tried to kiss me," she commented. "He always does say how irresistible I am. He's gonna love this."

"I'll just bet he is," I said absently, wondering if there was any way I could resign from the two jobs I had. I hadn't asked to be an animal interpreter *or* to be a detective. Surely there was some sort of rescind clause, I thought hopefully.

But I already knew how it worked in Gales Haven. A witch had no say in what magic she developed. And what Bessie Gawama said, went.

I hadn't asked for the assignments, but I was stuck with them both nonetheless.

CHAPTER SIX

"WANDA'S SHOP IS MY FAVORITE," Aunt Luanne told me as she pulled open the door and breezed inside, Aunt Shawna right behind her.

"I'm not sure that bodes well," I mumbled, fully aware of the occasional crudeness of my childhood friend's sense of humor. Besides, what else would a Cock, Coffee, and Cocoa Café be about other than cock, coffee, and cocoa?

"Your aunts are a hoot," Jadine said, sweeping past me and into the establishment, doing little to allay my unease.

When I stood there staring at the now closed door for a moment, and the words etched across it with magic, glittering and shining brightly, Mindy said, "What are you afraid of? The cock, the coffee, or the cocoa?"

I snort-choked. "I'm not afraid of any of them."

"Then why are you just standing here? You had your panties in a knot you were in such a hurry to get here, and now you're paralyzed with fear."

"I am not." Then I shut my mouth. Again, what was the point? I swung the door open so hard, I slammed it into my other shoulder, the one the tiny tyrant didn't occupy. Swallowing a grunt lest I give her more fodder to taunt me about imagined weaknesses, I swept into the café while telling her, "And my panties were so *not* in a knot. I don't even usually wear panties. I prefer to go commando."

The door swung shut behind me in a hushed silence that could only mean one thing.

Of course everyone had heard me. What else should I expect to happen on a day like this one?

I smiled tightly and searched for my aunts and Jadine. I found Quade instead.

His whiskey eyes twinkled with amusement. "It's nice to see you, Marla."

I tilted my chin high. Okay, so everyone in the shop, which was very busy, knew I wasn't wearing undies. So sue me. No biggie. It wasn't like I wasn't wearing pants.

"It's nice to see you too, Quade," I said, mature as can be.

"Good way to cover up your discomfort," Mindy told me. "I'm sure he already forgot about your panty situation with that great howdy-doody you gave him."

I did my best to ignore her. Too bad I was wearing the hedgehog.

"What are you up to?" Quade asked me while cradling a tall steaming mug.

"Oh, the usual. You know, playing pet detective, almost literally."

"What?" He looked very confused. Welcome to the club. So was I.

"Nan says I'm to be the new town detective. Apparently, I get zero choice in the matter. And I have a hedgehog on my shoulder who won't stop telling me what to do."

I smiled tightly. I must look like a maniac. At least the outside was matching the inside.

"Also," I forged ahead, "I have my first case. Jadine thinks a leprechaun is stealing her Spanx and then cutting the crotches out just to mess with her. So, despite the fact that I'd rather be doing just about anything else, I'm here to pick up Wanda, because Nan says she needs to be on the case too, and then we're going to go find a leprechaun and force him to hand over the crotchless Spanx."

Quade blinked at me. I blinked back. Yup, I was letting all the crazy hang right on out there.

"So, how's your morning been?" I asked with a *Looney Tunes* smile spread across my face. If I was going to have to say shit like that, I was gonna own it.

"Oh, you know." His blank stare morphed into a mischievous grin that blinded me to everything but him for a few moments. "Nothing too exciting. Got Harlow to school. Picking up a cup of coffee before I head over to the library. I'm going to be working on the landscaping there for a bit."

"I see." The tension eased from my shoulders until Mindy tightened her grip on me, and I clenched all over again, hoping she hadn't snagged my sweater yet. It was purple with sparkly silver threads woven in. It was soft and fuzzy *and* it was flattering to my figure. I loved it.

"So your forest magic is still going strong?" I asked Quade.

"It is." His eyes twinkled, and this time I knew it was due to his love of nature. He adored everything that grew from the earth. "I've fine-tuned my magic a lot since you've been gone. I'd love to show you what I can do sometime."

"That sounds great. Once I finish solving this caper?" I tried to keep a straight face. I failed.

He chuckled. "Absolutely. In the meantime, I'll do what I can to forget about your panty-less comment."

Our gazes met and heated. He obviously had no

intention of forgetting about my comment. Quite the contrary.

"I can probably get out of my detective duties right now," I half-joked.

He laughed, the gold of his whiskey eyes flashing. "Well, if you can, you know where to find me. But somehow I doubt you're going to be getting off that easy…"

"Yeah, I doubt that too," I muttered miserably. The panty-less part of me was fully on board with the idea of playing hooky, however.

He moved closer and leaned toward my free shoulder, whispering, "I can't wait to have some time to catch up with you."

His words weren't particularly romantic. But the heat of his breath made a warm shiver race across my body. The memories of what time alone with him was like made me flush all over.

"I can't wait either," I said.

He placed a feathery kiss on my cheek and disappeared through the door.

"Wow," Mindy said. "Way to play it cool."

"What do you mean?" I thought I had been pretty cool considering I'd announced to the whole establishment what my choice in underwear was.

"You were all breathy like, 'Ooh, oooh, Quade. Do me now.'"

"Wait, what?" I tried to look down at her, but she

was too close to my face for me to focus properly.

"You heard me."

"I was so not like that. And where did you learn to talk like that anyway?"

She shook her head. Or I thought she did anyway. She was blurry.

"I told you, I can go anywhere, overhear anything. I know more about the people in this town —and how they talk—than you probably want to know."

"There's no probably there. I definitely don't want to know what most people in this town get up to."

"I don't blame you. They do some freaky stuff when they think no one's looking."

I waited for her to continue. When she didn't, I couldn't help myself. "What kind of freaky stuff?" Blame my curiosity, not me. She couldn't dangle that carrot and not expect me to chomp down on it.

"Oh, you wouldn't believe. You know Darnell Adams?"

"Of course I do. What about him? What's he do?"

"Marla!"

Wanda's voice cut across the café, drawing my attention to my wild, dark-haired friend behind the counter.

"Hey, Wanda." I smiled and set off in her direction. "We're going to have to table this gossip-fest," I whispered to the tiny shoulder-rider. "I want to know what Darnell does."

"I might not be in the mood to tell you later," she said, sounding petulant.

"You, moody? Nah."

"Are you making fun of me?"

"Oops. No time to talk. Wanda's waiting for me."

I could feel her stare on my face as if it were a tattoo gun. I ignored her and opened my arms to hug my friend.

"Hey, girl," Wanda said, careful not to squish Mindy as we embraced. "What are you up to? This is quite the posse you're hanging with. Are you looking to get into trouble?"

"Why?" I chortled. "'Cause you want to join in?"

She laughed with me. "You still know me." She glanced at Mindy. "Seriously though, what are you up to?"

"I'll get to that. First, let me check out your place. You run it all by yourself?"

Wanda beamed. "Yep. I have people who help me cover the shopfront of course, but as far as making all the big decisions, it's all me."

Scanning the place, I took in the glowing candles positioned across most surfaces, lending the large open room a warm ambiance. Like all candles affected by magic, they appeared to burn continuously without melting down the wax. Light wood paneling surfaced the walls, and overstuffed armchairs of different colors dotted the room amid small round tables and an eclectic collection of chairs and art—mostly nude paintings a la Gustav Klimt. No one thing matched the other. It was exactly as I imagined Wanda would be if she were a room.

"I love it," I breathed.

Shelves lined the longest wall, filled with all sorts of books, small and large. Figurines of roosters hung from the ceiling. Made from wood, ceramic, fiber, straw—every variety of material—there were dozens of them. Some were painted, some were plain, but every single one of the ornaments dangling from the ceiling was a rooster.

A cock.

"I finally get it," I said. "When I first saw the name of the place..."

"Your mind went right to dirty thoughts." Wanda sounded quite happy of the fact as I nodded. "That's exactly what I was going for!"

"You wanted people to think: 'Come have coffee or cocoa in my sex toy shop?'" That seemed a bit much, even for Wanda.

"Of course I did! Sex sells, even in Gales Haven."

"But you're not really selling sex, right? Of any kind?" With Wanda, it was worth triple checking. She was right, I knew her too well...

"No, of course not." She waved a dismissive hand

around her shop.

Luanne, Shawna, and Jadine were at the bar ordering some drinks. I heard the faint *cha-ching* ring out, indicating that their purchases were being recorded in the ether by the commercial ledger that kept tally of all the residents' purchases.

"Out here, it's all legit," Wanda added.

I stared at her. She was practically bouncing she wanted me to ask so much.

I debated whether to string it out and torture my friend. But I figured I owed her. I'd been gone for a very long time. I'd effectively left her too.

"What about not 'out here'?" I asked, and her lips pulled into a smile so wide, I could see her gums—top and bottom.

"Well, you didn't think I'd have a boring shop, did you?"

"I don't think it's boring at all. I think it's lovely. I want to hang out here all day. Honestly, I'd live here if you'd let me."

"And give up Jowelle's cooking? I don't think so. I might be good, but I'm not Jowelle good. No one is, except for maybe Bab. Though I do hold my own in the quiche department especially. My quiches are to die for."

"Well, I hope no one does die over them, or Nan will put me on the job."

Wanda raised her dark, perfectly arched

eyebrows in question.

"She says I'm the next town detective."

Mindy chuffed atop my shoulder, like I couldn't possibly be good at the job. Though I probably agreed with her, I proceeded to ignore her fresh reminder that I had a tiny critter on my shoulder.

"What do we need a detective for?" Wanda asked, ignoring Mindy too.

I sighed. "Stolen Spanx. It's a long story. Don't make me tell it."

"Oh, I will. You can't tell me that and then not tell me the rest."

"Okay, well then, I'll tell you as we go. According to Nan and Jelly Frumpers, you're supposed to help me solve this mad caper. We need to find a leprechaun. Maybe."

She barked a laugh.

When I looked properly miserable, she said, "Oh, you're serious."

"Unfortunately."

"Leonie," Wanda hollered, unmindful of her customers. None of them seemed to care. The atmosphere was relaxed and friendly.

I hadn't spotted Leonie, and yet she materialized out of somewhere, wearing a flour-dusted apron and her usual creepy pigtails that moved like they were snakes attached to her head.

"What's up, boss?" Leonie asked while I worked

very hard to keep my attention on her face and not her hair.

Wanda asked her, "Can you cover for a bit while I go help Marla? She's on official council business and they need me."

Wow, Wanda made it sound so much more important than it was. She always did know how to spin a story.

"Absolutely," Leonie said while the dozens of braids surrounding her head undulated hypnotically.

"You're okay covering the back room too?" Wanda asked.

"Of course. I've got it all covered. Is that what Luanne and Shawna are here for? The back room?"

Suspicion tugged at my toes. "What's in the back room?" I totally didn't want to know, and yet I totally did.

"I want to know too," Mindy said. "I've never been able to get back there or to confirm the rumors were true."

"What rumors?" I asked her.

"What do you mean, what rumors?" Wanda asked.

"I was talking to Mindy. The hedgehog," I deadpanned, because none of this was weird, right?

"Oh."

"So ... what's in the back room?" I pressed.

Wanda giggled. "What do you think your aunts might be interested in?"

I groaned. "Maybe I don't want to know."

Leonie beamed at her boss. "The Cock, Coffee, and Cocoa Café offers the best selection of sex toys in all of Gales Haven."

Wanda smiled at her employee fondly. "We also happen to offer the only selection of sex toys in Gales Haven."

I looked at the both of them, then at my aunts, who did appear to be shooting sketchy glances at a door in the back corner I hadn't noticed before.

It was painted a scarlet red, with a gradient of gold glitter beginning at the bottom and fading as it reached the top.

If ever there was to be a door to a magical back-room sex toy shop, this was it. It didn't need lettering to announce its purpose.

Aunt Shawna and Aunt Luanne were giggling together, and it looked like they were pulling Jadine into the mix. Before I could be indirectly responsible for whatever they were telling Jadine, I snapped my attention to Wanda.

"So are you in or are you out? Because I have to get my aunts out of here before they try to walk through that door."

"It's trippy through there," Leonie said.

"Trippy?" I asked, utterly confused. "How can sex

toys be trippy?"

"Oh," Wanda said. "You didn't actually think I'd have a kink shop, did you? There are no wall displays of dildos or vibrators to be found, my friend. I'm talking spells and enchanted objects, obvi."

"Obvi," I parroted, wondering if perhaps I was dreaming. *That* would explain a whole heck of a lot.

"You definitely should check it out," Leonie said, braids flapping around excitedly.

"I'll take a rain check." Rain checks never had to be cashed, after all, not unless curiosity got the best of me.

"You got it, my friend." Wanda rubbed her hands together excitedly. "I'm so ready for an adventure. Life got a little boring without you here."

"Well, I somehow doubt there's gonna be a boring thing about our caper solving."

"Awesome." She grinned those gums at me again. "So, what are we looking for?"

"Not sure yet. Maybe a leprechaun wearing crotchless Spanx?"

"Got it. See ya, Leonie. Bye, everyone," she called over her shoulder as she walked toward the front door.

Only Wanda Woodles could take a possible leprechaun wearing pilfered Spanx in stride. That's why she used to be my bestie. I was hoping she'd want to fill the role again.

CHAPTER SEVEN

"WELL, THIS IS ANTICLIMACTIC," Jadine commented to Aunt Luanne, Aunt Shawna, Wanda, and me, and even though she couldn't talk back, perhaps also to Mindy, who scampered off my shoulder the moment we arrived at Jadine's small bungalow. The hedgehog definitely nicked my sweater on the way down, yanking out some of the awesome sparkly purple yarn so that one sleeve was now sporting the polka-dot effect. I tried hard not to hold it against the tiny creature but failed.

"I figured you'd be detecting," Jadine added, and this time her comment was directed solely at me.

I shrugged. "Hey, I'm not the one who decided I should be a detective. I'm wholly unqualified to fill the position."

"Not if Bessie said so."

I smiled tightly. "Of course." Because Nan said I was to detect, I was stuck with the role whether I liked it or not.

Sitting back in my chair around Jadine's round dining table, I studied her kitchen. It was homey and clearly well used. Cheerful paint brightened up the space, and fresh flowers gave it a crisp, floral scent.

"Do you have anything extra to add to our tea?" Luanne asked.

Gales Haven being the friendly place that it was, Jadine had offered us all tea—even the hedgehog, who declined via my interpreting—the moment we walked through her front door. And Gales Haven being the magical, easygoing place that it was, Aunt Luanne didn't have to specify what she meant. We all knew, probably even the hedgehog.

I cleared my throat. "Um, Aunt Luanne, don't you think we should keep a clear head for this caper-solving business?"

"Um, no," she said right away.

I waited for more explanation. None came.

I leaned forward on my elbows, nestling my teacup between the palms of my hands. "If you get *happy*"—I gave her a meaningful look as I referenced Mabel's Happy Times—"it will be more difficult to think straight."

No one said anything, though Jadine did get up

and start opening cabinets, pulling out small dropper bottles.

I tried again. "We need to keep a rational mind."

Luanne *tsked*. "Since when has a rational mind helped a damn thing? We're in Gales Haven. Have you forgotten how nutty things can get around here?"

"Nope. I definitely haven't."

"I'm not so sure."

"Aunt Luanne, are you serious right now? I'm a *mad caper detective*, and I'm sussing out a *leprechaun. Who's possibly stealing and mutilating Spanx.*"

Enough said, am I right?

"You just proved my point," she said. "There's nothing normal about what's going down. So why should we be normal? Shouldn't we make ourselves as un-normal as the caper we're trying to solve, so we're at the same vibration of it?"

I chuckled despite myself as Jadine returned to the table and deposited five violet glass dropper bottles on the table in front of her.

I said, "Aunt Luanne, there's no danger of you ever being normal, even without Happy Times."

"Marls, I'm not talking about Happy Times." Everyone but me and Mindy laughed. "You don't put Happy Times in tea, silly goose."

"You've been gone a long time," Aunt Shawna said. "Mabel's come up with all sorts of other concoctions that are milder than Happy Times so you can use them throughout the day. You know, when you still need to get stuff done."

Jadine was nodding. "She's right skilled, that Mabel, and we need all the help we can get to solve this crime. And we need to get moving before the trail grows cold."

"The Spanx trail," I deadpanned.

She nodded eagerly some more.

"Right." I forced a smile. When faced with so much crazy, perhaps Aunt Luanne was right and rolling with it was the only way to go.

After all, it wasn't like lives were at stake here. We were talking Spanx, not the barrier spell now. Nan and her team were dealing with Delise's magic, not me, so what was I worried about? Worst case scenario, Jadine lost out on a few Spanx. She'd live. We all would.

"Okay," I said, starting to see my crazy aunts' side of things. "What have you got?"

Jadine held up the first little bottle and Mindy climbed up to the back of a chair to get a better look.

Jadine pointed at her with the bottle. "Go no further. No animals are allowed on my eating table."

Mindy growled.

"Did she just *growl* at me?" Jadine asked.

"Yep. She doesn't like to be called an animal."

"Then what on earth does she want to be called?"

I shrugged. "A magical creature. It's a fair description. I mean, she can talk."

"Right." Jadine gave Mindy a wary side-eye before returning her attention to the bottle in her hand. "This one's called *Smile, Child*." She put that bottle down to pick up another. "This one's *Groovy Moves*. I really like this one." Again, she exchanged bottles. "This one's *Sleep Without a Peep*. Yeah, not this one. How about *Let Loose* or *Think No More*? These both sound just about right for what you're looking for, Luanne."

Jadine waved around both violet bottles, the late morning sunshine filtering in through the windows of her kitchen to make the color of the glass deep, rich, and mesmerizing. Forget the contents, I wanted the bottles.

Luanne reached for them. "I'll take both."

"Me too," Shawna said.

"Really?" I scrunched up my face with dubiousness. "You both are already loose." I paused to listen to what I'd said. I hadn't meant it *that* way, but the description still fit. "And I really do need you to help me think. I haven't the first clue about how to be a detective."

Mindy chuckled.

I whirled on her. "What?"

"A detective finds clues, and you don't have any."

She laughed some more, the sound like a metal utensil tapping china.

"I didn't ask for this job."

Aunt Luanne sounded serious for once: "None of us get to decide our jobs. The magic decides for us. You know that. It's no use to complain. Just suck it up, buttercup, and get on with it. I've got a hot date tonight I don't wanna miss."

She added a whole dropperful from one of the bottles to her tea while she spoke, and then passed it over to Shawna. Next she unscrewed the top from the second bottle.

They were going to do whatever they wanted, of course they were. It's what they always did.

I said, "I have to get Clyde and Macy from school long before you have to worry about your hot date."

"Oh, I'm not worried about it. I'm looking forward to it," Aunt Luanne said.

"Maybe you should come by my shop to pick up a little something extra for it," Wanda suggested. Her rich brown eyes twinkled in delight as she observed our interactions.

Luanne grinned. "That's a great idea."

"I think I'll do that too," Shawna added. "I could do with a hot date."

"Oh-kay," I butted in, pretending like none of all that had just gone down. "Jadine, show me where the stolen articles went missing." I wasn't sure how many more times I could say *Spanx* and keep a straight face.

Jadine popped up from her chair. I remembered Jadine quite well from my high school days. She'd been a firecracker then and I doubted that had changed. If anything, the residents of Gales Haven got wilder as they got older. I had proof all around me.

"You gals go ahead," Aunt Shawna said. "We'll enjoy our tea."

"Good idea," Aunt Luanne added. "She's the detective anyway, not us. Hmm. This tastes so good."

Wanda giggled and brought her own cup to her lips, staring at me over the rim. She at least hadn't added anything to her tea.

I allowed Jadine to lead me to a laundry room off the kitchen and pretended to register everything she said as she shared inane details about her laundering habits. Nodding politely, I sipped at my tea, forcing my mind to stay focused.

When she showed me the slices of fabric that had previously constituted the crotch area of her Spanx super-high-waist undergarments, I worked hard not to appear grossed out. She kept rubbing the fabric in her fingers as she spoke, growing more agitated, while I tried not to think about where the scraps had last been.

By the time we returned to the kitchen, Aunts

Luanne and Shawna looked like they'd just had the best sex of their lives. Their wild hair was mussed, their eyes glazed and unfocused; perma-smiles tugged lazily at the corners of their lips.

Wanda looked like whatever had gone down in my absence had been funny as hell. Her mouth twitched with mirth; her eyes were bright and brimming with amusement.

I was busy wishing I'd been there to see whatever my aunts got up to instead of listening to Jadine drone on when I noticed Mindy was gone.

"Where'd she go?" I pointed to the chair back the hedgehog had last been perched on.

Luanne and Shawna shrugged while Wanda frowned. "I didn't notice her leave, sorry. I was distracted."

My aunts whispered something to each other and cracked up with infectious laughter.

Yeah, I would've been distracted too.

"She's gotta be in the house. Mindy!" I called out.

"Actually," Jadine said, "she could've gone out the flappy door." She pointed at a pet door at the bottom of her back door that I hadn't noticed earlier.

"Do you have pets?"

"No, but I want to be prepared in case I ever do."

In this town, it was as good an answer as any.

I went over to the pet door and pushed on it. It gave easily. It was possible Mindy could have slipped out this way. But why would she want to? Especially without telling me first? Mindy always had something to say.

Swinging the back door open, I froze when I spotted a quill on the deck of the porch that wrapped around the back of the house. Bending down, I picked it up and examined it. It was the right size and color to be Mindy's. But no matter how long I stared at it, I couldn't deduce another thing. What had Nan been thinking assigning this job to me?

Then I spotted a torn scrap of black shiny fabric, partially shredded, a few feet away. It reminded me of satin...

"Jadine?" I called through the open door behind me. "Is this a piece of your Spanx?"

She and Wanda poked their heads out. Jadine's eyes widened. "Dammit, it looks like it."

"I take it you didn't put it out here?"

"Hell no. I told you, I take mighty good care of my Spanx. It's only fair as I expect them to take good care of me. I never dry them outside. Never. The only time they come outside is when I'm wearing 'em."

"Don't tell me you're thinking whoever took the Spanx took Mindy," Wanda told me, expression dubious.

I rose to my feet, quill in hand. I wasn't touching any part of Jadine's Spanx. "I'm not sure, but maybe. I have no idea why anyone would want to take Mindy though. She's kind of a pain in the butt."

Wanda shook her head at me. "You only think that because she talks to you. To the rest of us, she looks cute as a button."

"I could see that." I pushed the hair back from my face while I thought it over. "Maybe this is just a scrap from the earlier theft and Mindy just left without telling me."

"Nope, it's not from earlier," Jadine cut in. "I swept my porch just this morning. And trust me, I would've noticed evidence of this heinous act if it'd been here then."

I sighed. "Yeah, I don't think Mindy would have left without telling me anyway. Not when Nan assigned her to the task. She wants to be a representative of the magical creatures on the town council. It'd be a stupid move not to take part in the town's issues when Nan asked her to, and in no way is Mindy stupid."

"You think whoever stole Jadine's Spanx came back just now, while we were all here, and stole the hedgehog?" Wanda asked, brow furrowed in incredulity.

"It seems pretty insane to think it, I agree," I said. "But yeah, I'm considering it. It doesn't make a lick of sense, but it could be what happened."

"It makes sense to us," Aunt Shawna called out from inside the house.

"Yeah," Aunt Luanne added. "Maybe the crime dude came back to see if there were any more Spanx to steal"—Jadine gasped in affront—"ran into Mindy who was outside—"

"Maybe she had to tinkle," Shawna interjected.

"Makes perfect sense," Luanne continued. "And the dude found her, thought she was adorable because he can't hear her talk like you can, and took her."

"Because he thought she was adorable?" I asked through the open door, from where I could see that my aunts appeared to have drained their tea—and Mabel's medicinal herbs.

"Exactly," Luanne said while Shawna nodded and beamed at me.

I threw my hands in the air. "Well, seems as good an explanation as any. So now we're maybe solving the mystery of the missing Spanx *and* a missing hedgehog."

Wanda grinned. "Sounds fun."

"I'm pretty sure Mindy won't think it's fun," I muttered.

"Oh, don't worry so much, Marls. This is *Gales Haven*, remember? I'm sure she's fine. She probably just took off. It's not like she needed a permission slip to leave. She's a creature, not a child."

"And the scrap of Spanx?" I asked.

She shrugged. "Who knows? But nothing bad ever happens here."

Jadine scoffed. "Excuse me?"

"Nothing *seriously* bad ever happens here," Wanda amended.

Even so, unease filtered through me as I considered the possibility, however slight, that Mindy might have actually been kidnapped. I was feeling strangely protective of the tiny magical creature whose hobbies included raising orphans and giving me grief.

Wanda was probably right. *Why* would anyone take her? There was no good reason for it.

Then again, there seemed no good reason for stealing Spanx either...

Mindy must have left on her own and shed a quill on her way out. It wasn't like she was the most patient of creatures. She could have grown bored of waiting for me while Jadine droned on about her precious Spanx, and decided to mosey on out on her own.

Then the doorbell rang, pulling me away from my worries, and because it was a magical doorbell that wasn't actually electronic but governed by a small spell, it sounded like charging horses were racing toward us. Despite my knowledge that we weren't about to be mowed down by a stampede, I still flinched and held on to the porch railing for good measure.

"I'm coming," Jadine hollered and crossed the kitchen in the direction of the front door.

"You hear that?" Aunt Shawna giggled. "She's coming."

"Maybe all she needed was to loosen up the hold those Spanx things had on her crotch," Luanne responded, mischief animating her face. "So she could loosen up all over."

My aunts laughed at their inappropriate line of thought as I heard Jelly Frumpers' voice at the door.

I released my hold on the railing and entered the house, Mindy's quill still in hand.

If Jelly had more predictions about me, I was liable to slam the door right in his face.

CHAPTER EIGHT

JELLY WAS much as I remembered him. Even as a teenager, he'd been round and grumpy. Now, he was even more so. A pot belly hung over his pants, straining the limits of his button-up shirt. Small flashes of flesh peeked out from the gaping holes between buttons. His nose and mouth were scrunched together in bitter lines.

My first thought when I saw him was, *Crap, what now?* The second was, *Why wouldn't he go see Mo Ellen about a spell?* Just as soon as I solved this caper, I was literally running to see her. For one, I could really use a nice run to relieve some of the stress of all the happenings since I'd arrived in town. But mostly I just wanted free rein to eat *all* the food—and not end up looking like Jelly.

When he lived in a place replete with magic,

where he could literally eat whatever he wanted and not balloon out like he was nine months pregnant with twins, why would he want to look like he did? More so, why would he want to *feel* like he must looking like that? There was no way he could bend over or even see his toes. He probably had to fumble around just to find his limp noodle.

Ew. No. I was so not going there.

"Marla," he said by way of greeting, dragging me away from thoughts I had no business having.

"Hi, Jelly," I said.

"Whaddya want, Jelly?" Jadine asked, better matching his level of friendliness.

"Bessie Gawama had one of her feelings that I'd find Marla here. She says Marla listened to me and is solving crimes now."

Theoretically, I'd been more or less ordered to play detective, but I didn't suppose I had to tell him that. Though his sour attitude really made me want to. Still, he could tell a bit of the future. I didn't think he had any control over what happened, but it seemed safer not to mess with the curmudgeon. I didn't need him reading itchy rashes or monstrous zits into my future just to spite me.

"Yeah, so?" Jadine said. "Why are you here?"

I wondered if she and Jelly had history of some sort. Jadine was far from being sugary sweet, but this outward aggression wasn't like her either.

Jelly pushed his chest forward, which meant he ended up pushing his sizable belly out too. "I thought the new Gales Haven detective would want to know that I just saw the leprechaun I predicted was going to be in town."

I sidled up to Jadine. "You actually saw the leprechaun?"

"Sure did." He struggled to stuff his hands in the pockets of his pants, also tight on him, but he managed it, grinning a bit smugly. "Saw him running by with a bag of loot clutched in his hand."

I sighed. "A bag of loot?" I'd been hoping I'd be able to solve the Case of the Missing Spanx before picking up my kids from school, but now there was Mindy. And if there was even more...

I rubbed a hand across my face.

"I knew it," Jadine snarled, spinning to face me. "I knew that leprechaun would be up to no good, none at all." She side-eyed Jelly, then spoke through the corner of her mouth, speaking just as loudly as before, but giving me something to chuckle at. She was no good at all at discretion.

"I bet that leprechaun's carrying around my ... you-knows ... in that bag of his."

"What are your you-knows?" Jelly asked right away.

"Dammit, Jelly," Jadine snapped. "I wasn't talking

to you. I was being all discreet-like. You weren't supposed to listen."

"But you were talking right in front of me."

"And a polite person wouldn't have listened."

"But—"

Jadine cut him off with a hand and a look that would've shut me up too. "My you-knows are none of your business."

"Then why are you saying *you*-knows? That implies I should know, because when you're saying *you* it's actually me."

"No, Jelly, *you* is never *you* when I say it. You can bet on that."

If they kept going like this, my brain was going to tie itself into a pretzel. "Jelly, where did you see the leprechaun and what did he look like?"

Wanda walked up behind me to listen in, but Aunt Luanne and Aunt Shawna's laughter filtered in from the kitchen. They were useless as detective's aides or whatever Nan sent them along to be.

"If we're going to talk, can I come in?" Jelly asked Jadine.

"You should bloody well know the answer to that, Jelly," Jadine answered right away, convincing me they definitely had some sort of history together. "Whatever you have to say, you can say it from my front steps."

"Fine." He huffed, then gazed out into the

distance for a moment before focusing on us again. "Wanda." He nodded at Wanda, and she nodded back. "I was walking back from my appointment at Hair for Hotties & Hatties..." he began.

When Jadine opened her mouth, I pressed an elbow into her ribs. If she kept dragging this out, I was going to lose my mind. Jelly was all but bald, and not by choice.

"It's such a nice day that I decided to take a stroll and head on over for a treat at Three Hundred Sixty-Nine Fabulous Feisty Flavors. The special of the week is cherry chocolate and that's my favorite."

With effort, I forced myself not to yell at him to get on with it already.

"I was eating my triple scoop ice cream, with chocolate syrup and nuts on top, while I walked, taking my time. We've been enjoying such nice weather lately, I didn't have anywhere I needed to be just then. I hate it when I have to rush and be some-where. It puts me in a bad mood."

My right eyelid twitched. I was starting to regret not having added shots of Mabel's concoctions to my tea.

"There were a lot of people walking around when I was."

"Oh my knobby knees, Jelly," Jadine, who had round, not knobby knees, growled. "Get on with it already. Some of us do have places to be!"

He scowled at her. "I was on Magical Main Street, almost at Moonshine Park, when a leprechaun streaked by, carrying a bag behind him." He crossed his arms, leaning them on his belly. "There, are you happy?"

"I'll be happy once you're not darkening my steps," Jadine said.

"What did this leprechaun look like?" I asked for the second time. "And how are you sure he was a leprechaun?"

"I guess I can't be one-hundred-percent sure," he said, "but since I saw a leprechaun coming with my future-telling magic, and this guy was tiny, red-haired, and sprinting by me, I figured that's what he was. I almost dropped my ice cream when I saw him. Thankfully, I didn't. It'd be a sin to waste all the chocolate cherry."

"So how tiny is tiny?" I asked. After all, I'd been dealing with Mindy lately.

"I'd say he'd come up about to mid-thigh on me. Maybe he was shorter. It was hard to tell he was moving so fast. He was also really skinny, like he only ate once a week. His hair wasn't quite as red as yours." He pointed to my curls. "It was more orange-y."

"Got it," I said. "And how was he dressed?"

"Oh, that's what was really interesting. The rumors about leprechauns have it wrong. They don't dress in button-down green suits with shiny black shoes. And they definitely don't wear hats." His face scrunched up in confusion. "But I didn't think they'd dress like this either."

We waited for him to continue on his own, but he didn't, lost to his memories.

"Jelly?" I prodded before Jadine could rip his head off with her bare hands.

"Oh, right. It looked like he was running around buck naked but for a black shiny thing hanging from him. A shirt or something. You could even see his butt cheeks hanging out from under it. When he ran, the shirt lifted up and, boy, did I get an eyeful."

Jadine narrowed her eyes at Jelly in place of the leprechaun. "How shiny was his shirt? Like satin shiny, like plastic shiny, or another kind of shiny?"

"I'd say like satin shiny. The whole getup looked pretty decent on him, I suppose. If the alternative was a stuffy green suit, I'd probably do the same."

I swallowed thickly. There was no way I wanted to imagine Jelly running around buck naked but for Jadine's Spanx. And by now I was deducing that's exactly what the leprechaun was clothed in. From the depth of Jadine's scowl, she'd guessed that too.

"I'm gonna kill him," Jadine said.

Jelly's hands shot up. "Hey, I'm just telling you what you asked to know. You can't kill me for that."

"Not you, ya eejit. The leprechaun. He stole from me."

"Oh." Jelly dropped his hands back to his belly, where they rested comfortably. "What'd he steal, then?"

"I won't be telling you now, or ever, so you'd best not bother asking."

He frowned. "But—"

Jadine leaned forward and glared at him so hard that he shut right up.

I was so glad I wasn't on Jadine's bad side...

"Did you see where he went?" I asked Jelly.

"He ran into Moonshine Park, of that I'm sure, but he was going so fast I doubt he'll still be there. I went to find Bessie right away though. Well, after I finished my ice cream of course."

I smiled lamely at him. "Of course. Could you tell what he was carrying in the bag?"

"Not really. Now that I think about it, the bag might've been made of the same material as his shirt. I couldn't see through it at all. Though it did look to be moving a bit."

"Moving how?" Wanda asked.

I followed up, tensing all over: "Like something alive might be in it?"

His eyes widened. "Yeah, exactly like that. Like something was bouncing around in there. You think he had something alive in there?" His eyes bulged. "Is he a rotten kidnapper?"

He looked to me for an answer. But for all I knew, Mindy might be squirreled away somewhere safe and sound with her many children and her not-all-there husband. I was starting to seriously doubt it, however. Making itself at home in my gut was the unpleasant feeling that Mindy was exactly what was writhing around inside the leprechaun's Spanx loot sack.

"Is there anything else you can tell us that might help us find the leprechaun, Jelly?" I asked.

"No, that's it."

Jadine slammed the door in his face.

"A thank you would've been nice," he shouted through it. "I went out of my way to come over here."

"No one asked you to come," Jadine yelled through the closed door, and Wanda and I backed away.

"Well, it'll be the last time I do anyone a favor. Do good, and look what it gets you."

"You didn't do us a favor. We didn't want you here. Now go away."

"Finally you ask me to do something I want to do. You're freaking nuts."

"Then you made me that way 'cause you were nuts first."

Jadine's fists bunched at her sides while she waited for a response. But none came.

"That wanker," she growled, turning toward us. "He knows how much I hate it when he doesn't let me keep fighting. Of course he'd just walk away! He's trying to drive me crazy."

Pursing my lips together so I wouldn't reveal my true thoughts on the matter, I exchanged a look with Wanda while I waited for Jadine to calm down on her own.

My friend clapped a hand to her mouth so she wouldn't laugh. A giggle escaped, and I lost it just like we used to when we were teenagers, known for laughing at the most inappropriate moments. But was there any better stress relief?

I bent over at the waist, laughing.

Until Jadine said, "You'd better not be laughing at what just went down here."

I tried not to laugh so hard that I choked.

"Did you and Jelly have a fling?" Wanda asked, undeterred by the murderous eye daggers Jadine was throwing our way.

Jadine tipped her chin up. "Maybe we did. I told y'all I'm husband hunting."

"Woman," Wanda said, "if you think Jelly is good husband material, you need to think again."

"Why?" she accused. "'Cause he's round? Round people deserve love too, you know."

"Of course it's not because he's round. It's because he's grumpy. He's always in a bad mood. This was the happiest I've ever seen him."

"That's because he was seeing me. He's been trying to see me for weeks, but I've been turning the other way whenever I see him on the street."

"You make him happy?" Wanda blurted out, sounding shocked.

Jadine blushed. "I think so."

"Wow. Okay, then. How 'bout that? Never thought I'd see the day Jelly Frumpers would be happy. Good for you guys."

Jadine scowled. "Oh, there is no us. No way. He's an ass."

"I thought you just said..." Wanda trailed off.

"I know what I said, and I never said he wasn't an ass."

"Alrighty then," I jumped in before things could get out of control.

Who was I kidding? Things were already out of control, and I hadn't even started hunting down a bare-assed leprechaun.

I made my way into the kitchen, calling as I went. "Aunt Luanne? Aunt Shawna? You ready to go?"

They looked up, mildly glassy-eyed, but looking so happy I couldn't blame them for it.

"Where are we going?" Shawna asked.

"To find a leprechaun who's apparently wearing

Jadine's Spanx as a shirt. We need to get Mindy back."

Shawna gathered her empty cup and her sister's and walked them over to the sink. "And how are we going to find him? Didn't sound like Jelly knew where he was now."

"No, but someone in town must have locator magic. Who?" I asked, excited that this idea just occurred to me. I was starting to get used to thinking in terms of magic again.

Luanne waggled her lips left and right while she thought aloud. "Well, Dixie can locate all sorts of things. I'm not so sure about people though. Wait, are leprechauns people?"

"I have no idea at all what a leprechaun is," I said, "but I am sure he's trouble. Trouble I'm so not in the mood for."

"Oh, come on." Wanda patted me on the back. "Drop the hard-ass act. You're having fun."

"No, I'm not."

"Yes, you are."

"Am not."

"Are too."

In a huff, I turned on my heel and stomped toward the front door, all the while trying to hide the smile tugging at my mouth.

Maybe Wanda was right. Though if I was having fun, I really needed to better define the term.

And I knew just who I'd like to help me with that. But I had to solve this caper before I could focus on Quade Contonn. Once I had time alone with him, I didn't plan on anything interrupting us. We had lots of missed time together to make up for.

CHAPTER NINE

DIXIE LIVED a few blocks down the street from Jadine, so we decided to walk there. Aunt Luanne, Shawna, Wanda, and I waited for Jadine to lock up her house—with its absurd amount of deadbolts—while my aunts made faces behind her back. Every time Jadine would turn to look over her shoulder at them, they feigned innocence. I was a spinoff of Snow White stuck with the reject dwarves, Dumpy and Stumpy.

Whatever was in Mabel's tinctures was good stuff. I'd have to make time to stop by her shop soon. My aunts weren't taking a single thing seriously. I was totally jealous. They were having so much more fun than I was.

Nan had saddled me alone with the responsibility of detecting. Since Jelly's fortune telling was what gave her the idea, I'd have to thank him for that one later. She hadn't assigned my aunts a specific role, they were just along for the ride—and they were turning it all into one big carnival.

Or maybe that was just life in Gales Haven.

Jadine flipped through her loaded keychain, searching for the key to what I prayed would be the final lock.

"People in town don't even have locks on their doors, and those who do don't bother locking them," Wanda said. "Why in the dickens do you have a gazillion of them?"

Jadine *tsked* as she narrowed in on the correct key and slid it into the third deadbolt that lined her front door. She had four on her back door. "Did you forget that I'm the victim of a *crime*? Someone broke into my house—invaded my privacy and sense of security —and stole my belongings. Of course I installed protection as soon as I discovered the crime."

I was pretty sure referring to stolen Spanx as a crime was stretching it—pun only mildly intended.

"As soon as I discovered the criminal act, I sent Danny a whisper-tell, asking him to come right over with his tools."

Wanda arched a brow. "And did you barter with something? In order to make use of his *tools*?"

Jadine flushed and fumbled her key ring, bending over quickly to retrieve it, before stalking down the steps. Without waiting for any of us, she set off along the street in the direction of Dixie's house.

Wanda exchanged wide-eyed looks with my aunts before the three of them giggled and started after Jadine.

I hurried to catch up to them. "What am I missing?"

When Wanda turned to me, her face was alight, fully animated, eyebrows dancing. "Oh, Danny's been known to cut you a break on barter exchange if you include some *shugah* in the trade, if you know what I mean." She winked at me in an exaggerated manner.

No, I didn't know what she meant. What kind of *sugar* was she talking about?

I watched the way Jadine all but speed-walked ahead of us on the old tiled sidewalk. "Are you telling me that Danny does work in exchange for sexual favors?" My pitch rose as I started to get agitated by the idea. "'Cause if so, that's really not cool. That's downright pervy, Wanda. How could you guys let this go on?"

My aunts bent over at the waist laughing. Aunt Luanne waved my concern away. "Oh it's not like that. Danny's a hottie."

"So? Being a hottie doesn't excuse a dude from being a perv! He can't trade out..." I glanced around us, saw no one else, but lowered my volume just the same. In Gales Haven, someone was always trying to be up in your business, even if you didn't spot them. "He can't trade out sex for handyman work or whatever he's doing."

"Oh he's *doing* at least a dozen ladies in town at any given time," Aunt Shawna said, and Aunt Luanne leaned a hand on her sister as she wheezed with laughter.

I crossed my arms over my chest and glared at all three of them, not caring that Jadine was leaving us behind. We'd catch up.

"I can't believe you. How is this okay to any of you?"

Wanda ran a finger beneath her eyes to wipe the moisture from all the laughing at me they were doing. The more worked up I got, the funnier they thought it was.

"It's really not like that—promise," Wanda said, still grinning. "Danny's hot as flames, but that obviously wouldn't have us standing by while he's doing something wrong. He's a sweetie. He isn't coming on to women who don't want him to."

Aunt Luanne clutched at her stomach. "Oh my funny bone, my belly hurts from laughing so hard. I really needed that."

I frowned at her. "Seriously? So what, Danny's some gigolo and you're all okay with it?"

Aunt Shawna wrapped an arm around my shoulders and set us walking again. "There are more women than men in this town. Some of them get lonely when they don't have boyfriends or husbands. Or lovers."

"Or when they don't know how to please themselves without a man!" Aunt Luanne called ahead to Jadine, making me cringe at the thought of how many people might have heard her. We were walking along a quiet little street that was perpendicular to Magical Main Street and lined with quaint homes.

Shawna, completely unbothered by Luanne, nodded. "Danny offers these women a little adventurous fun."

Wanda drew up to my other side. "Your aunts are right. He offers them some fantasy, and they eat it up. Many of them literally."

"Ooh, good one, Wanda," Luanne said from behind us.

"They're all grown women," Wanda added. "They know what they want and how to get it. Danny isn't forcing them into anything. He's just offering them a taste of what they're desiring."

Aunt Luanne giggled in delight. "They lap him right up."

"All right. That's enough of that." I again shot

surreptitious glances at our surroundings, though it didn't do much good. There were definitely people eavesdropping. I'd bet that was one thing that hadn't changed a bit during the years I was gone. "But him offering ... it up ... in exchange for work and payment, that feels off."

Wanda smiled gently at me, the laughter gone now. "You've been away for a long time. You've got to remember that here there aren't any real bad guys. Even Delise and what she did to the barrier spell, I'd bet anything she didn't do it with malice. She probably didn't think past her ego long enough to realize what she was doing was really going to harm the town."

"As much as it pains me to think well of Delise in any way whatsoever," Shawna said, "I agree. She probably just lashed out 'cause she was angry with Nan for not letting her on the council. I think she just wanted to add her magic to the spell so they would need her."

Grimacing, I arched my brow at them. "Uh, did ya see her? She was nuts!"

Shawna shrugged. "Delise has always been a bit nuts. Most people in Gales Haven are. But most everyone else is lots nicer than she is."

"And a bazillion times more fun," Aunt Luanne added.

"Well, excuse me if I'm not in the mood to forgive her," I said.

"Who said anything about forgiving her?" Shawna asked. "I hope Irma really is stringing her up by her toes."

"Or waterboarding her," Luanne said. "That would be good too. Maybe ripping her fingernails off."

I scrunched up my face. "Ew, Aunt Luanne. That's a bit much when you just finished saying she didn't really mean to sabotage the barrier spell."

Luanne walked next to Shawna and shrugged. "Either she's stupid as a bag of rocks—and I don't mean the smart talking kind like what Troy sells in his Toys, Trinkets, and Tinies shop—or she's evil. Either way, we shouldn't let her get away with what she did. Oh! We could electroshock her. It'd be funny to see her hair standing up all over her head."

I opened my mouth to censure my aunt, and then figured why bother? Sighing, I said, "Well, so long as Danny isn't pushing anything on anyone, then I guess I'll let it go."

"When you see Danny, *you* might even be asking him to come install locks on your door." Wanda smiled at me so broadly that I couldn't resist a chuckle.

"I don't even remember him," I said. "How old is he?"

"Just old enough for a saucy woman like me to not feel bad about taking him up on keying me."

I whipped my head around to Aunt Luanne so fast that I didn't watch where I was going and tripped over a raised tile edge. Wanda and Aunt Shawna caught me while I gaped at my youngest aunt. "Aunt Luanne, are you being serious right now? Did you really have sex with Danny?"

Luanne shook her head at me, her wild red hair tumbling around her face. "Why does your mind always shoot straight to sex?" She blinked at me, deadpan. "Oh, that's right. 'Cause you're related to me."

I inhaled deeply and wondered what could have possibly made Nan think sending Luanne and Shawna along with me on this caper solving was a good idea?

Luanne leaned across her sister. "'Course I had sex with him. I'd be crazy to turn him down. I had several servings of that yumminess."

"He came on to you?" I asked.

She shrugged. "Oh who knows? Him, me? It's all the same. We had fun, that's all that matters. Actually we had lots of fun. Maybe I should dip into that well again. How about you, Shaw, did you go there?"

Aunt Shawna opened her mouth, and "Hey," I interrupted, before we could go further down this path. As it was, whenever I met Danny, I'd probably turn beet red and get tongue-tied. I didn't need that. I already had to live with the fact that everyone in town knew me and Quade were on the way to getting back together. I didn't even know what was up with us yet, but I could tell everyone was just waiting to find out.

Searching for something to say, I spotted Jadine on the front porch of a cute little lilac house up ahead. "That must be Dixie's house," I announced, relieved to have landed on something with which to distract everyone. "Jadine's already knocking."

"Oh no," Shawna said as we watched a woman who must have been Dixie open the door to Jadine. Jelly Frumpers was directly beside her, inside her house—standing a bit too close to her.

"Are Jelly and Dixie good friends?" I asked hopefully.

"Nope," Wanda said.

"How about cousins?"

Dixie was taller than me, voluptuous in that hourglass way, and pretty. Jelly was short, round, and definitely not pretty.

"I've never even noticed them talking before," Wanda answered.

I couldn't see Jadine's face from where we walked, but if Jadine had behaved like a jilted—and crazed—lover at her house, how was she going to react to seeing Jelly with another woman?

As if Wanda and my aunts were arriving at the exact same conclusion, we picked up the pace, climbing the steps to Dixie's house in no time.

We arrived just in time for the standoff.

My money was on Jadine.

CHAPTER TEN

"HIYA, DIXIE," Jadine said with a tight smile before turning her ire on Jelly. "And what are you doing here, Jelly? Just dump one woman and skedaddle right over to the next? That's your style now, is it?"

Dixie's mouth dropped open as she brought a hand to her chest. "My word," she whispered, looking between Jadine and Jelly.

Then she stepped next to Jadine—and away from Jelly, who was now on the receiving end of two murderous glares.

Jadine flung her key ring to the ground in anger, then brought both hands to her hips while she huffed like a wild beast.

Dixie, who was revealing her smarts with every passing second, took another step toward the panting bull on her doorstep, making sure we all got her message loud and clear. Whatever Jelly did, he was on his own. Dixie was hanging him out to dry like he was laundry.

"What'd the man do to you?" Dixie asked Jadine. "Because I tell ya, he and I haven't done a thing together. Sure, I was thinking about it, but only 'cause we've got a shortage of good men in this town. If not, I wouldn't have gone there. No way."

When Jadine turned her panting focus on Dixie, the woman barreled on, trying to fix what she'd said.

"I mean, no way am I going there now, not after this, and I haven't done anything with him. I'm all spent after Danny came by to fix my shower."

I gasped. Danny again.

Jadine looked about ready to blow. I wouldn't have been surprised if steam shot out from her ears like in the cartoons. She scraped the wooden steps with a boot like she was a bull pawing at the dirt beneath him before he charged.

I had no idea how this would go, but I was certain of one thing. A whole bunch more drama was about to go down.

Efficiency was not a quality most people in this town were afflicted with, and I didn't want to continue bobbing and weaving without getting much accomplished. I had a life to live beyond mad capers, Spanx, and bare-assed leprechauns.

Jadine stomped toward Jelly, getting right up in his face.

I walked up to her and placed a hand on her shoulder.

She whirled on me, fists raised.

"Whoa there." I released my grip on her.

"Sorry, Marla. I got nothing against you. I'm just strung tight is all. This jerkwad's been bouncing me around like an idiot."

It was unclear whether she meant she was the idiot or he was. I was going to apply her statement to both of them.

"It's okay," I said. "But before this goes down, I've got to jump in. I have a case to solve, as you well know, and I mean to solve it as quickly as possible. So will you hold off on letting Jelly have it until we get what we need here?"

"Hey!" Jelly protested.

We all ignored him.

"Sure thing," Jadine said, her flared nostrils settling a bit.

Nodding at her, I faced Dixie. "Hi. I'm Marla Gawama."

"I know who y'are, hun. Everyone here knows."

"Right." I smiled, but it didn't reach my eyes. "I'll lay it out nice and simple. I have a case to solve. There's a leprechaun in town who's stealing stuff and animals—I mean, magical creatures—and I need to stop him. I've been told you have locator magic. Can you locate the leprechaun for us?"

"Sure I can."

I sighed in relief. Maybe I'd wrap this up before the end of the day after all. "Awesome. How long will it take you to tell us where he is?"

"Not long. A few days."

"A few *days*?" I spluttered.

"Yeah. I can do spells to find objects much faster. But if you need one to find a person, it takes longer. And if you need one to find a magical type of being, then I'm figuring it's gonna take longer still, though I've never done it before. The more complex the thing or person I'm finding, the longer it takes to get the spell just right."

"What if you were to locate one of the things he's stolen?"

"Then it'd go faster. What'd he take?" Dixie twirled a strand of her long, dirty blond hair and waited expectantly.

But I didn't want to answer her. Not in front of Jelly and Jadine, who didn't want Jelly to know.

"Um, Jelly?" I started.

"What?" he growled like he was a grumpy bull-dog, with none of a bulldog's cuteness.

I wasn't sure how to phrase this diplomatically, so I just came right out and said it. "Will you go?"

When the sides of his mouth dipped even

further, making the resemblance to a bulldog more accurate, I added, "Please."

"Why should I have to leave? I was here first."

That was the breaking point. I lost what little control I had. Smiling dangerously, I said, "I don't care that you were here first, just as I don't care who you're dunking your dipstick in."

Dixie winced at my crudeness. Behind me, Aunt Luanne chuckled.

"You can keep doing whatever you want *after* I do the job I'm here to do. All right?" No one spoke for a moment. "I'm only here because my nan, Bessie Gawama, asked me to figure this crap out. So let me do what I need to do before I lose whatever sanity I have left listening to your squabbles. Got it?"

I gave Jelly my crazy-woman look—eyes narrowed, teeth bared, hair wild. I was sure I looked unhinged.

He stared at me, his own nostrils flaring with his anger, until he finally nodded once. Then he stepped out of the house, "accidentally" bumped Jadine on the hip as he stomped by, and walked between us women as we parted to make way for him.

"Oh no he didn't," Jadine seethed.

"Oh yes he just did," Wanda said, like she was enjoying the show.

"Go get 'im," Aunt Luanne told Jadine in the pitch one reserved for pets.

Jadine huffed down the steps with such fury that the wooden planks shook even with the rest of us standing on them. When she barreled down the sidewalk, Jelly turned and noticed her. He increased his pace to a brisk walk that wasn't really all that swift. Jadine waddled after him.

"That's not gonna work out too well for him," Aunt Shawna commented.

"No, it's not," Wanda said. "Her legs are a lot longer than his. She's gonna catch him."

"Hmm, I don't know," Aunt Luanne said. "He's awfully motivated, and though her whole body's shaking, she's not going all that fast."

Jelly Frumpers cast frequent glances over his shoulder as though a guard dog were chasing him. His stubby arms pumped at his sides and his breathing came too heavily; I could tell even from Dixie's front porch.

"Jadine's gonna get him for sure," I said. "He's got too much of a belly."

Mesmerized by the scene, we all stood there and watched. Jadine's hips were wagging to each side so precariously I worried she was going to throw one out. She placed a hand against her side as if she'd already gotten a stitch.

"Jadine needs to start working out," I observed as Jelly cut across the street, Jadine close to catching him. She followed across, then he looped back around, and started heading back our way, face bright red.

"I can see why she thinks she needs the Spanx," Wanda said. "Everything's jiggling."

Jadine's butt and thighs were like a Jell-O mold in action as she stormed after Jelly.

"I still wish she'd love herself just the way she is," Aunt Luanne said. "It's no good for a woman to criticize herself."

"Agreed," Wanda said.

"We'll have to have her over sometime for a counseling session," Aunt Shawna said. "Self-love will fix a lot of her problems."

"Oh!" I gasped, and we all—even Dixie—winced as Jadine tackled Jelly to the sidewalk.

"That's gotta hurt," Dixie said.

It had to have. Jelly lay writhing on the ground, not getting up.

Jadine straddled him.

"Is she gonna hurt him or...?" Dixie's question trailed off.

I grimaced. "I really don't know."

Jelly had flipped onto his back under her, and from the looks of things, he'd stopped resisting.

"Maybe we could step inside to discuss things?" I suggested.

"Good idea," Dixie said, but didn't move to make room for us.

None of us moved. It was like a car accident, where you really didn't want to look, but you couldn't seem to help yourself.

Neither Jadine nor Jelly did much ... until Jadine slammed her mouth against his.

"Oh," Dixie squeaked.

Jadine and Jelly really started going at it, making out in the middle of the sidewalk.

"All right. Time to get inside," I said.

Nodding fervently, Dixie backed into her house, opening the door wide. But her eyes never left the scene unfolding almost directly across the street from us.

The rest of us followed suit, backing in.

When Dixie closed the door behind us, I exhaled loudly. "Thank you. I didn't want to watch anymore but it was like I just couldn't stop myself."

"Same," Wanda said.

My aunts, Wanda, Dixie, and I stood crammed in the vestibule to the small house for a bit before we snapped ourselves out of it.

Wanda shook her head as if clearing it. "That was oddly mesmerizing."

"Like watching reality TV," I said. "You really don't want to watch, and then four episodes later, you have no idea what happened."

The women stared at me blankly.

"Ah," I said. "Right. No streaming here." Gales

Haven had DVDs. Anything that didn't require an internet connection. I'd even spied some old VHS tapes in the family room at Gawama Mama House.

I'd forgotten how much I'd enjoyed leaving town to go to the movie theater with Quade when we'd been younger. It had felt like a special outing to go into the next town over since we had none of that here.

Again, I digressed. My mind kept chasing squirrels, and I was starting to get hungry.

I ran my hand through my hair, remembered it was pinned up, dropped it, and said, "Dixie, can you track Spanx?"

She snort-laughed. "Is that what the leprechaun stole?"

I tried to be serious about my detective role ... but failed. "Yep. He stole five pairs of them."

"And they're Jadine's?" Her eyes were wide with greed. Without really knowing her, I understood that gossip was one of her main food groups.

"Yes," I said, without elaborating. I had no intention of embarrassing Jadine while she was outside mauling the face of the most ill-humored man in town.

But Dixie's eyes glittered. She backed up expertly on rhinestone-covered heels I wouldn't wear unless my life depended on it, and teetered over to an archway that led into another room. "Let me just grab my spell stuff. I can get right on it."

"Great, thanks."

When she returned with lavender-colored sheets of loose paper and a small wooden humidor sized for cigars but certainly filled with something else, I asked her, "What's it going to cost me?"

I hadn't been gone from town long enough to forget how it worked here. No money was used. There was no credit or debt. Noreen Bradley, the scribe for the council, doubled as recorder and accountant. Whenever someone wanted something big, say a house, they went to see Noreen. She signed them up for a house—either to purchase or build—in exchange for bartered hours of work. Noreen made it all happen, maintaining an intricate ledger of who did what and for how long until they satisfied their agreement. Once Noreen struck the original arrangement, the ledger updated the rest on its own. A spell updated the tallies as the work hours were completed. There was no cheating the system.

Dixie's exchange with me wasn't important enough to warrant inclusion in Noreen's ledger, but it wouldn't come free—especially since she wasn't a friend.

Dixie considered me while the rest of us waited. Since according to my aunts she was the only one in town any good at this, she had me up against a wall. I just hoped she didn't realize it.

"You know what?" she finally said. "Let's call it even. You just saved me from what I'm pretty sure would have been a big mistake. I don't need the problems of Jadine, and after seeing her and Jelly together, I for sure don't need him either."

"No offense, Dixie," Wanda started in the way one did when whatever was coming next was at least somewhat offensive. "But what were you thinking? Jelly is no match for you."

"I am much prettier than he is."

"You are, but that's not what I meant."

She shrugged. "Guess I should've asked Danny to stay instead, huh?"

"I'd bet you would've had more fun," Aunt Luanne piped up, and I hurried to divert the conversation. I so could not handle the thought of this Danny as a lover to both Dixie and at least one of my aunts.

"The locator spell?" I prompted. "I'll take the deal. Thanks." I smiled.

"You got it." She smiled back. "So the spell will take me a while to craft..."

"How long?"

She shrugged. "Like an hour or two at most. Their accuracy improves remarkably if I let them stew a bit. But you don't need to be here while that happens."

"Oh, good," I said on a sigh. "I could use some lunch."

"Your Aunt Jowelle's food?"

"Yep."

"Lucky you."

"Definitely. How about I bring you some takeout when I pick up the spell?"

"Deal. But you can just drop off some goodies whenever you're in the area. I don't need you to come back for the spell. I'll send you a whisper-tell when it's done."

"Okay. So how does it work?" I asked. Wanda and my aunts were attentive, meaning the effect of Mabel's tinctures was already starting to wear off.

"I'll link the spell to you, Marla. Once the spell is active, you'll feel a tug, like intuition, leading you toward the object. In this case, the Spanx." She snickered.

Thankfully, the rest of us didn't, so we could get this done already without any more of my aunts' laughing fits.

"You'll be able to follow this feeling toward the Spanx until you find them. Once you locate them, the spell will end. It's a onetime thing."

"Got it," I said. "Anything else you need from us now?"

"Nope. I'm sure there isn't any other stolen Spanx in town for my magic to get confused with. I'll start as soon as you leave."

After more thanks and promises to deliver Aunt Jowelle's food someday, we did leave, but we snuck out like burglars, peering through a cracked-open door before pulling it open all the way.

Jadine and Jelly were gone.

There wasn't a chance in hell I was going to go looking for either one of them. Whatever they were up to, I was very happy not to be a witness to it.

CHAPTER ELEVEN

THOUGH I INVITED Wanda to join my aunts and me for lunch at Gawama Mama House, she declined and left to check on Leonie instead. Apparently whenever Leonie had to go into the back room to assist customers, she was liable not to come back out again in any reasonable amount of time.

Since Aunts Luanne and Shawna were with me, I doubted Leonie would have cause to go into the back sex spell room—whatever it actually housed. Then again, apparently several women in Gales Haven considered Danny-time one of their favorite hobbies.

Maybe Wanda was right in thinking Leonie would be stuck in the back room while her café went unattended.

Regardless, Wanda promised me she was only

taking a rain check, and that she'd be coming around to hang out with me all the time—like when we were younger. She made it sound a bit like a threat the way she leaned into me when she said it, as if I weren't going to have a choice in the matter.

Luckily, I was looking forward to time with Wanda. We'd been thick as thieves before I left town, and whenever Quade and I hadn't been locked away for alone time, which was often, we all hung out together, laughing our tails off at Wanda's latest antics. We laughed even harder whenever she managed to rope us into them, and harder still when we ended up in trouble.

As my thoughts turned to Quade, I sighed contentedly—amazed. Quade Contonn. I never imagined I'd have another chance at happiness with him...

Nan's chuckle cut through my reminiscences. "Leave her be. She's got that starry-eyed mooning look about her."

Shaking my head to clear it, I looked over at my nan. She looked tiny seated at the head of the table, but her smile was wide, making her appear decades younger. This was the Nan I remembered and most loved. She was alight with life. I hoped she'd live forever, though death was one event witches had learned never to mess with—it rarely went well. But those with magic could live longer than regular humans; it all depended on what kind of power they possessed and whether it fueled their longevity. I had no idea whether Nan's magic would extend her life by decades—after all these years I still hadn't managed to pin down exactly all of what she could do—but she had her wily ways, so I was definitely hoping.

I didn't want to have to do without my Nan. Ever. She was the bedrock of this family. Of the town.

"See?" she told the others. "She's daydreaming."

"About Quade I'd bet," Aunt Luanne said from across the table from me.

"Hey, what?" I said.

Nan, my three aunts, and Everleigh, who was Nan's guest for lunch, all laughed. Aunt Jowelle scowled.

Aunt Shawna leaned onto her elbows to peer at me from beside her, both brows raised. "You're telling us you weren't just thinking about Quade Contonn?"

Aunt Luanne waggled her brows. "And how handsome he is? And all that he can do with that fine body of his?"

"Holy hell nuggets, Aunt Luanne," I said. "Does it always have to be about sex with you?" I leaned back to encompass Shawna in my next statement. "Life can be fun without everything being about sex, you know."

Even as I said it, I wondered if I would have if

Quade and I'd had a chance to get fully reacquainted.

I expected Luanne or Shawna to begin preaching about the benefits of sex and why being sex-crazed was better than being just plain crazed, which, according to them, was a real danger if they didn't squeeze all the fun they could out of life. What I didn't expect was for Everleigh to be the one to comment first.

Everleigh, with her eternally long, shockingly white hair, leaned forward from next to Aunt Luanne. She locked eyes with me. I'd never noticed how light hers were, or how unique. They were a blue so pale they appeared violet. She pinned me with them, and I wondered if she could see right into my soul.

"You're forty-four, yes?"

I blinked in surprise. "That's right. Though I'd rather you not rub it in." I alone laughed awkwardly.

"Aging is nothing to be afraid of."

"I'm not afraid—"

Her mouth spread into a cat-ate-the-canary grin, telling me flat-out she thought she knew me better than I knew myself. I had no idea whether she might be right.

"We women are like wine," she said. "We get richer and finer with age. We discover the subtleties of our taste. When you learn to really honor your desires, you're free. When you decide you don't give a flying fart what anyone else thinks of you or what you do, then you're free as a wild bird."

"Heck yeah," Aunt Shawna said, and Aunt Luanne nodded her head, silently saying, *Preach, woman.*

Aunt Jowelle *tsked*. "Behaving with self-respect and dignity is even more important."

Everleigh smiled at her sadly, as if Jowelle were missing out on the point of life. Biting my lip, I had to agree with the crone who gave me the willies while simultaneously making me want to follow her to the end of the Earth.

Maybe she was right.

Everleigh said, "The way we have true respect and dignity for ourselves is to honor the true song of our spirit. That means not holding back, but letting our true selves come forward."

"But that doesn't necessarily have to be … *sex*."

Aunt Jowelle pronounced the word like it was foul. Was she that traumatized over not being able to conceive a child that she associated her disappointment with sex? Why else would she hate the act?

I hadn't enjoyed really good sex since the beginning of my marriage to Devin, when I threw myself into our relationship with the assumption that connecting in a physical manner would overcome the lack of true heart connection between us. Even so, I hadn't forgotten how great sex could be. I hadn't forgotten what it was like to share myself fully with Quade.

"You're right," Everleigh told Aunt Jowelle. "You don't have to have sex to fully express or honor yourself. We're all completely different, and as such, the same situation will have varying results in different individuals. What's important is that we not hold back out of fear. Fear will keep you from living life. Once you aren't afraid of what anyone thinks of you or what you do, you'll feel thirty years younger. And once *you* don't judge yourself for what you do, you may as well be a kid all over again. That's when you really and truly start living."

Damn, I wished I'd recorded that. That way I could replay it every time my mind wouldn't shut off when I thought about Quade—and most everything else I did and then often doubted afterward.

Aunt Jowelle's scowl was gone, replaced by an absent look in her eyes, suggesting she was deep in thought as well. Hopefully dreaming and not regretting.

"I couldn't have said it better myself," Nan told Everleigh. "Life is meant to be lived. The more outrageously, the better."

Everleigh beamed at my nan. "No wonder we get along so well."

"Damn skippy," Nan replied.

I sighed contentedly. My nan and Everleigh were well on their way to fulfilling my badass-crone-bestie fantasy. No way would these two not get into trouble —the best, empowering kind. I was going to love watching their friendship develop.

Taking a bite of Aunt Jowelle's pasta salad— penne mixed with arugula, capers, Kalamata olives, fresh shavings of Parmesan, and a decadent dressing —I forced myself to focus on the caper I was supposed to be solving. It took force of will to direct my mind where Nan apparently wanted it.

I'd only just arrived in town. I wanted to be settling in, taking my time, helping my kids adjust, not jumping from one fire I had to put out to another.

"I hope Dixie hurries with that locator spell," I commented. I'd already filled everyone in on what had gone down that morning. "That leprechaun could be anywhere by now."

"At least the break gave you time for a nice lunch," Aunt Jowelle said. "It's no good to skip meals."

I smiled warmly at her. "Especially not when the food is as good as yours. This salad is delicious."

"It really is," Everleigh said. "When Bessie invited

me for lunch, I couldn't pass up the chance at one of your meals."

Aunt Jowelle preened like a male peacock—all without moving but a few inches. Even seated, she somehow grew taller. Her face glowed with the grin she was trying to swallow.

"Thank you," Aunt Jowelle finally said. "I give it my all."

"That you do, my dear," Nan said. "And we're all so grateful."

Thankful mutterings circled the table. Aunt Jowelle looked like she could die right then and be happy for all eternity.

"How's it going with the barrier spell?" I asked Nan and Everleigh. I really hadn't wanted to ask. I hadn't forgotten how Harlow told me I'd be needed to remove Delise Contonn's magic from where it hooked into the barrier spell. I was hoping she was wrong. I'd already had enough of being the town's quasi savior.

Nan frowned, and she rarely did that. "It's not going great. Delise's magic isn't reacting well to being pulled free of the barrier spell."

Everleigh, the strongest of the spell weavers, who was leading the efforts to untangle Delise's magic from the oldest, and most important, spell in town, frowned too. I doubted she did that often either.

"Every time I pull the thread of her spell away, it

just slips free of my grasp and clings to the barrier spell. It's like it's bonded to it, which it shouldn't be."

"And that's a big problem, I gather?" I said.

"A huge problem. We're all getting tired out of trying the same things over and over. Scotty points Delise's threads out to us, and Kama and I grab them and pull them away. They slip out of our hold like rubber bands snapping back into place. The other spell weavers have stopped trying. It's just Kama and me now."

"So what else are you going to try?"

"Who knows?" She speared a large mouthful of pasta and arugula. "We'll keep at it until we figure it out or Irma brings Delise back. Then we can torture the solution out of that pink-loving punk." Everleigh chewed, unaffected, like she really intended to torture the woman we all loved to hate.

No one else at the table protested the plan, especially not Nan, even though she was the one person at the table who could have forbidden it.

"When you finish solving your current case," Nan told me, "I'd like you to come by the entrance to town and take a look. Maybe there's something you can do to help."

And I hadn't even told her what Harlow said...

"The barrier spell is still stable though, right?" I asked. "Delise's spell isn't advancing any further, and the town's protected, yeah?"

"Yeah." Nan narrowed her eyes at an imaginary Delise, the skin around them crinkling. "But I don't trust that woman for a second. The faster she's out of the spell, the sooner she can be gone from our town. And then I'll be able to sleep again. I've barely been sleeping, and a woman of my age needs her beauty rest."

When I passed her room last night, I'd heard her snoring, loud as a chainsaw. Still, with how fierce she looked right then, I wasn't about to tell her.

"You're planning on exiling Delise?" Aunt Jowelle asked, stilling me. I hadn't thought Nan was serious. No Havener had ever been exiled. Not in the long history of the town.

"I plan on doing whatever needs to be done to protect our town. I'm sure the rest of the council will agree with me."

I was sure they would too. Did that mean Quade and I could share a future without Delise poking her nose in our business at every turn? The thought of being with Quade just became even more appealing...

Everleigh grunted around another mouthful. She was on her second serving of pasta salad and gave no impression of slowing down. "If that woman's going to attack the town, then it's only right that the town protect itself by eliminating the threat."

"Exactly," Nan said.

A warm preternatural breeze circled me, and I straightened, anticipating what would come next. A hazy glow, much like a small puff of cloud, settled in front of my face. A moment later, Dixie's disembodied voice spoke from the center of the mist.

"The locator spell is ready. Follow the tug in your gut to the Spanx." A giggle wafted from the whisper-tell in a visible puff. "Good luck finding the leprechaun."

The cloud dissolved slowly, until it disappeared entirely.

"Well," I said, taking another quick bite of my lunch. "That was faster than expected. I've got to go." I speared a few more bites of pasta and shoveled them into my mouth, standing while I chewed. "I need to finish this up before Clyde and Macy get out of school. I want to be there to pick them up."

Nan waved away the idea. "Let them take the bus. No teenager wants their mom to pick them up from their first day of school. We did the part we had to. Everyone knows the kids are Gawamas. Now let them be."

But Nan was wrong. I would have loved to have my mom pick me up from school as a teenager. At any age, actually. I wanted to be the mother to my kids that I'd always wanted. I wasn't perfect, but I was doing a fine job. They knew they could rely on me for anything.

I picked up my plate and walked to the sink. "I'm going to go get them. I didn't even tell them to take the bus." I also hadn't told them to wait for me. Crap, I hadn't been thinking, complacent in how safe the town was and how easy it was to navigate it.

"Harlow will help them figure out what to do," Nan assured me. "Besides, Gus needs something to do. He isn't suited to much else. Driving the bus gives him a job. Let him drive your kids."

"Gus?" I said. "I don't remember a Gus."

"That's because you were gone a very long time, my Marla. You can't remember everyone. Besides, we've all changed in your absence."

I couldn't help but experience her words like barbs lashing against my heart. Had I hurt them how my mom had wounded me? I couldn't bear the thought! Though I wouldn't allow myself to regret my actions. Everleigh's advice still circled my mind, inspiring me not to get bogged down in all the crap that can keep you from really living.

Forcing myself past all the apologies and explanations I wanted to issue, I said, "And this Gus, is he okay to drive the bus?"

Nan scrunched her face at me. "Of course. Why wouldn't he be?"

"Because you're making him sound like a big dolt."

"Ah, well he is that. But he has a love for anything that drives. Driving the bus is perfect for him."

"Yep," Shawna said. "It's probably the only thing he could do."

And in Gales Haven, everyone was required to contribute to the capacity of their skills.

I slid my plate, scrubbed clean, into the drying rack next to the sink. "Fine. They can ride the bus. But if I find this dang leprechaun before school lets out, I'm going to pick them up, at least for the first day."

I had an uneasy feeling that I wouldn't be solving this caper in the next couple of hours despite my intentions. Why? Because nothing had gone smoothly, or at all as I expected it, since I drove my kids through the barrier into town.

Spinning, I took in my aunts. Luanne and Shawna were still eating, appearing in no hurry.

"Aren't you coming with me?" I asked them. Nan had said they should.

"Nah," Aunt Luanne said. "We've got better stuff to do."

When Nan didn't object, I nodded. "All right. I'll see y'all later, then."

It wasn't like Aunt Luanne or Aunt Shawna had done a single thing to really help. I'd probably get this case resolved faster without them.

Without an idea of where to start searching for a

Spanx-pilfering leprechaun, I slipped into a light jacket and out the door. Laughter followed me out, and I resisted the urge to find out what they were all laughing at.

The sooner I solved this caper, the sooner I could move on to something less ridiculous. That was motivation enough for me.

CHAPTER TWELVE

I DROVE around town aimlessly for the better part of half an hour. There'd been no intuitive bursts of inspiration, nor any tugs of any sort on my gut. Other than the occasional gurgling as my body digested Aunt Jowelle's lunch, my gut was remarkably silent. I was wondering if Dixie's locator spell even worked when I decided to park and continue on foot.

"Maybe I should go get Wanda," I muttered to myself as I stepped out of my Subaru Forester. But I didn't want to ask Wanda to abandon her business when she didn't truly trust Leonie to hold down the fort.

Nan had said I should bring Wanda along to help me solve this case, but she'd also said the same about Luanne and Shawna. And she hadn't protested when the both of them decided not to join me after lunch.

If I didn't need them, then I probably didn't need Wanda either.

Surely I could do this on my own. I just didn't want to, mostly because I didn't want to hunt down a leprechaun in the first place.

"Where should I go?" I wondered aloud, hoping I wouldn't have to return to Dixie's to figure out how to properly use her spell.

Looking around, I noticed I stood in front of Bab's Bopping Boopy Bakery. Perhaps my intuition had led me here! I cheered right up. I deserved a treat for all my kickass work since I'd rolled into town.

I was known to say that Bab's baked goods were second only to Aunt Jowelle's, but that was only because, in a blind taste test, I wasn't sure who would win, and I'd die rather than admit that to Aunt Jowelle. The two women were fiercely competitive. The only reason they'd managed to avoid a bake-off was because Aunt Jowelle only cooked in Gawama Mama House and never traded a single thing she cooked.

Aunt Jowelle believed she should never profit from the gift of her cooking, that it wasn't respectable —though she did barter with her work on the mental body, without bothering to explain what made her two gifts so different in that regard.

Bab thought her magic was hers to use as she pleased and however benefited her most.

There wasn't a chance I was getting in the middle of this years-long fight. I wanted them both to feed me.

The very moment I pulled open the door to Bab's shop, the scents of incredible baked goods washed over me, making me inexplicably content. Before even gawking at Bab's offerings, I promised myself I'd go see Mo Ellen for a spell as soon as possible. I owed it to myself. As soon as Mo Ellen's spell was active, I was going to eat myself into a carb-sugar coma, and I wouldn't regret a second of it.

Bab's bakery was never empty for long. Though it was the lull in the middle of the day, three customers waited at the counter for Bab to attend to them.

"Hey there, Marla," she called out while she rifled through the display case, lining up a tray of her specialty Enchanted Hearts. Enchanted Hearts were basically her version of doughnuts, except that she used a sprinkle of her magic to shape them like a heart with a heart-shaped hole in the middle. As a teenager, I'd wondered what kind of enchanted hearts had holes in them. Happy hearts were whole, weren't they? Regardless, I'd wisely kept my trap shut. My sense of self-preservation had always been strong, and Bab's Enchanted Hearts were mouth-watering delicious.

"I'll be with you in just a second," Bab announced.

"Of course. No problem. Take your time," I said.

Bab eyed me while she continued amassing Enchanted Hearts, and then a Twisty Turtle, on a takeout tray. "Did you already have lunch?"

"Sure did." I smiled at her. "Just had Aunt Jowelle's pasta salad." Then I noticed the way Bab's eyes seemed to dissect me. "It was great." My smile trembled as I realized Bab was baiting me, but I didn't know what to say next.

"Oh, I see. So Jowelle's food left you unsatisfied?" Bab commented for all her customers. "You had to come to me to satisfy your sweet tooth, didn't you?"

There was no safe answer here. Already I feared I'd said too much. It would get back to Aunt Jowelle, and then she'd spend the next week cooking up a frenzy just to prove to herself that her cooking was better than Bab's.

For Bab's part, she would do her best to ply me with her sugary sweets so I'd take her side.

Visiting Mo Ellen for a spell so I could eat everything I wanted climbed even further up my to-do list. The competitive gleam was bright in Bab's eye.

The three customers glanced between Bab and me, waiting to see what I'd say. The competition between the two women was no secret in town.

To deflect, I singled out the one customer I recognized. "Hey, Suzy. How've you been?"

"Oh, I've been great, thanks for asking."

Bab handed Suzy her tray of goods, and Noreen Bradley's commercial ledger updated with an audible *ching*, which echoed its pleasant chime throughout the bakery. Noreen's commercial ledger was a lesser version of her principal one. It was fully automated, and it didn't keep track of the big items like houses or vehicles, which the town procured from beyond its boundaries with magically created dollar bills that the council administered for needs that couldn't be satisfied by Gales Haven's industry.

An invisible tally of goods received and given balanced out with professional services rendered in an effortless system maintained by a spell nearly as old as the town. Whenever someone got lazy, the council put a proverbial boot to their rear end and the issue was solved. Those were the kinds of problems the council was used to dealing with.

Not this do-or-die crap.

Then I sensed a tug on my intuition ... or my gut. I couldn't tell which. Was my body telling me it was ready for some heart-shaped doughnuts, or was Dixie's locator spell finally working?

"Bab, sorry," I called out, interrupting her as she took the next customer's order. "Do you mind if I go in the back really quick? There's something I need to check out."

"What could you possibly need to check out in the back of my bakery?" she asked, swiping several small loaves of bread and stuffing them into her customer's reusable bags. "It's clean as a whistle back there. I take great pride in how I keep my bakery running. Unlike others..."

Now that was a low blow at Aunt Jowelle, one Bab definitely knew wasn't accurate. The two women were equally anal retentive in how they maintained their kitchens. Their attention to detail was well known throughout the community.

I let it slide, pretending I had no idea who she was referring to.

"I'm not questioning you in any way whatsoever," I said. "Nan sent me on a mission to solve some *very minor* crimes that have happened."

The kidnapping wasn't at all a minor crime, even if the victim was tiny, prickly, and a magical creature. But I didn't want to alarm anyone. Real crime didn't happen in Gales Haven, not really.

"I just need to look in the back to see if, um..." I noticed all four people in the bakery staring at me. "Uh, yeah, I need to see if anyone's in the back."

Bab shoved the ready order at her customer, the ledger chimed, and she hustled back from around the counter, tightening the strap on her apron. "Are you telling me some *criminal* might be in *my* shop?" Her voice, never shrill, was shrill.

The man she'd given his order to hurried out the door. I didn't blame him one bit. I wished I could do the same. Suzy, however, clutched her baked goods to her chest and watched the scene unfold. Like most Haveners, Suzy liked to be in the thick of the action, collecting details to gossip about later.

"I don't know if there's anyone back there or not," I answered frankly. I couldn't decide if the urge to inspect Bab's prep room had anything to do with Dixie's spell, or if it was just some freak thing, possibly even a made-up feeling. "But if there is anyone back there, it's definitely not some mastermind criminal. It'd just be a..."

I trailed off, wondering whether Nan needed me to keep a lid on the whole rogue mischievous magical creature wandering loose around our town.

"It'd just be a what?" Bab pressed.

I eyed Suzy and the other customer, whose name I didn't remember. Both women were hinging on my every word and not bothering to hide the fact.

Pulling Bab close, I whispered, "I'm looking for a leprechaun."

Bab yanked back, eyes wide. "*A leprechaun?*"

Suzy and the other customer lapped up the secret. Suzy couldn't quite contain a smug smile, probably at the thought of how much of a gossip queen she'd get to be later on.

"You're telling me a *leprechaun* might be getting all up in my stuff?" Bab called out as she marched back around her counter and through a swinging door into the back.

The door swung shut behind her.

Blinking at the door for a moment, I skedaddled right after her.

"Wait!" Suzy said, but I didn't, slamming through the door ... and straight into Bab, who stood frozen still, staring ahead.

Grabbing Bab to keep her from pitching forward, I looked around her ... and also froze.

"What the...?" I whispered, trying to make sense of what I was seeing.

I knew exactly what I was looking at, there was no confusing it. But my brain scrambled to make sense of the scene nonetheless.

Bab brought her hands to her sides. "Tell me I'm not looking at a buck-naked leprechaun passed out headfirst in my sugar bin."

I grimaced. "Ummm. Technically, I don't think he's buck naked. I think he's probably wearing a shirt." I left out the part about what I suspected the shirt to be made of.

"I don't see no shirt. All I see is round little butt cheeks where they sure as shit don't belong." She paused. "I also see that leprechauns are anatomically correct."

Yeah, so did I. I whipped my gaze away, fighting the urge to stare. Leprechauns weren't even supposed to be real, and yet here was one in the flesh—*all* the flesh.

"You don't suppose he died in there, do you?" Bab wiped a flour-dusted hand through her peppered hair, leaving a smudge behind. "He isn't moving at all. How can he even breathe in there?"

"I have no idea. He's a leprechaun. Maybe he doesn't have to breathe." I shrugged, taking in the deep sugar barrel tilted upward at a thirty-degree angle beneath the butcher's block work surface, positioned for Bab's ease of baking. She'd probably dipped down to scoop sugar from her bin thousands of times.

Bare skinny legs dusted in orange body hair stuck out from amid the sugar crystals. The soles of his feet were dirty—from walking around barefoot, I presumed.

"I have a mind to murder the little man," Bab whisper-seethed. "My work area is pristine! He can't come in here and ruin all that. He can't mess with my bakery."

"He must not have gotten the memo," I mumbled. If I were the leprechaun, there was no way I'd mess with the likes of Bab.

She marched over to a rolling pin that rested on a gleaming copper surface and snatched it up, slapping it against the open palm of one hand. Now, Bab was around Aunt Jowelle's age, so upper sixties, but Bab still looked like she could pound the living daylights out of a leprechaun—or anybody. Her arms were muscled from all that kneading. Bab didn't believe in machines making her work easier. Like Aunt Jowelle, everything was homemade, with no shortcuts beyond those her magic provided. Bab's magic didn't cover dough kneading. A line of whisks hung from hooks above one of the counters. She even whisked by hand.

"Wait," I said as Bab reached for the leprechaun's legs with one hand, the other holding the rolling pin in the air above her shoulder.

"Do you hear that?" I asked.

"Hear what?" Bab hadn't even tried to listen, continuing to reach for the creature in her sugar.

"That. Don't you hear that mumbling?"

This time Bab did listen, but she still shook her head. "I don't hear a thing, Marla."

I was definitely hearing something. Straining to listen, I walked toward a large walk-in pantry.

"You'd better not tell me something's invaded my larder," Bab said. "If something's in there too, I'm going to rip this naked creature a new one."

Doing my best to ignore her and her hopefully

idle threats, I advanced on the pantry and placed my ear against the closed door. There was definitely someone in there. I could hear them.

With my heart thumping in my throat, I yanked the door open.

Mindy waddled out, looking unharmed, one of Jadine's Spanx high-waist briefs—with thigh compression—stuck to her quills. She dragged it behind her though the satin underwear was many times her size.

"Where is he?" Mindy snarled.

"Who?" I asked, though I must have already known.

"The filthy-mouthed leprechaun, that's who." She marched across the bakery, brow low in fury, lips pressed against her muzzle. "I'm going to rip him a new one for what he did to me."

What were the odds that both irate females would say the same thing? I chuckled ... until both of them swung their fury on me.

I pointed at the sugar barrel beneath the counter. "There he is," I told Mindy, not caring one bit that I was bowing to a hedgehog. She looked ready for war, and with Bab as her backup, or the other way around, whoever got to the leprechaun first, I wasn't going to do anything to draw their ire.

The leprechaun chose the wrong females to piss off. He was about to find out.

CHAPTER THIRTEEN

"WHAT'S that hedgehog doing in my kitchen?" Bab accused, swinging her poised rolling pin in Mindy's direction.

I leapt toward Bab, hands out. "No! Mindy isn't a threat. She's a victim here."

Bab and I turned to face Mindy, who was snarling at Bab.

"I am *not* a victim," Mindy snapped at me, making me realize she was actually snarling at me and not Bab.

Hands up, I swept between the two females. "Fine," I said to Mindy. "You're not a victim. Agreed. But this leprechaun did kidnap you, am I right?"

"That he did, the scoundrel. And he's about to regret his actions."

I faced Bab, hands still up. "Bab, this is Mindy.

She's the … head of the magical creatures in Gales Haven?"

Looking to Mindy, I waited for her nod. Maybe she had an official title among the creatures she'd rather I use, and with the way she was glaring at everyone, I didn't want to piss her off any further.

But calling her the head of the creatures mollified her some. She lowered her lips from her muzzle and tipped her little nose in the air.

"You can call me the head of them," she said. "Or their leader if you want."

I swallowed a chuckle at the rapid turn in her temperament. It wasn't enough that I had to deal with all the egos in town, now I also had to deal with those of every creature with the desire to chat with me...

"I heard about your new abilities," Bab told me, leaning around me to stare at the magical creature. "So this is the hedgehog who can keep all the rest of them in line, huh?"

"Yep," I said. "She's a fierce one."

Mindy preened.

Bab nodded at the creature in acceptance. "And this leprechaun kidnapped her?"

"Snatched her when I wasn't looking," I admitted.

"She's so tiny it doesn't look like she can do much damage—"

Mindy growled.

"But her grievances against him are as important as mine, so she can join me in letting him have it."

Mindy nodded as I grimaced, wondering what the full extent of their punishment might be.

Nan hadn't told me what she expected me to do once I solved this caper. Did she want me to take the leprechaun into custody? I had no idea and hadn't thought to ask. It wasn't like Gales Haven had a prison or anything, at least none that I knew of.

Certainly Nan wouldn't want me to stand around while the little guy got a beatdown. Then again, Nan could be as fiery as Bab and Mindy put together. Maybe she'd be joining them in seeking retribution … so long as they didn't seriously injure the bugger.

But nobody waited for me to give direction. While I was busy pondering the correct course of action, Bab and Mindy advanced as if they'd coordinated.

Lined up behind the sugar barrel, Bab waited for Mindy to give her a *ready* nod, then she yanked on the leprechaun's leg hard enough to guarantee he'd get sugar burn from the friction—all up his private parts.

He popped out of the sugar barrel with a howl.

With the rolling pin at the ready in one hand, Bab held fast to the leprechaun with the other, her biceps bulging beneath her shirt. He dangled upside down in her hold, his arms and Spanx-improvised shirt over his head—which left his otherwise gangly, naked body fully on display.

"Ow, me bollocks," he griped, confirming that here was yet another magical creature whose speech I could understand.

"Your *bollocks* have no business being in my sugar," Bab barked.

She could hear him too. So not thanks to my special skill set...

"In fact," she added, "your little bollocks have no business being anywhere in my kitchen."

"Me bollocks aren't little," the leprechaun protested in a heavy Irish lilt. "They be big as cannon balls."

"So long as the cannon is miniature sized."

"Shite. Ya don't need ta be so mean. I do too have cannon-sized bollocks, and ya can go putting me down now."

Mindy jumped up toward him, snapping her tiny jaws at him. The leprechaun whipped his head around to check out this new threat, couldn't make out a thing due to the way his attire ballooned around his face, and swiped manically at the Spanx until he could see.

Then he chuckled.

Without thinking, I took a step back. Dude was on his own if he was going to make fun of murderous Mindy.

"That thing's so tiny," he said.

"Yeah, like your penis," Mindy growled.

Bab didn't understand what Mindy said, but the leprechaun sure did. After struggling with the Spanx by his face some more, he glared down at the hedgehog.

"Ya'd best not be insulting me manhood."

"Then ya'd best not be insulting *me*." Mindy even threw in a head wag, putting the depth of her attitude plumb on display.

The leprechaun stared down at Mindy while his face grew increasingly red from the blood rushing downward. After a bit, he fought the Spanx around his head some more, then shouted, "Lemme down already."

"No," Bab said.

The little guy stopped resisting, allowed his arms to hang over his head, and sighed loudly. "Fine. Then whaddya want from me? What do I need ta do for ya to let me go already? Ya know I won't grant yer wishes if ya be treating me like this."

Wishes? What wishes?

"Me ma would have a fit if she saw me with me bollocks hanging out like this. It wouldn't matter none that she's been dead and gone for years. She always used ta tell me, *Don't ya ever get caught without clean knickers on.* At least I'm not wearing dirty knickers, I suppose."

He sighed theatrically another time. But if he expected pity from either Bab or Mindy, I suspected he'd be waiting for it a long while. Mindy was still snapping at him, though even when she jumped she didn't clear more than a foot of air.

"And what would she think of you kidnapping a magical creature?" Mindy accused as Bab added, "How'd your momma feel about you breaking into my bakery, then? Huh? Would she approve of that?"

"If you're gonna hang me upside down like this, the least ye can do is not make me dizzy talking to me all at once," he said.

But of course, Bab couldn't hear Mindy.

"I'm going to have to spend the afternoon scrubbing my kitchen now that you've been all over it," Bab said. "And throw out all this perfectly good sugar. I have half a mind to tie you up and let Mindy have at you until she's had her fill."

"Who's Mindy?" he asked, voice ratcheting up in alarm.

"The hedgehog."

"Oh." He laughed. "What a gobshite. Ya had me really worried for a second there."

Mindy growled so ferociously that the leprechaun lunged upward, trying to make a grab for his legs. He managed it and held on, casting anxious glances down at the miniature creature with an ire a hundred times her size.

Bab hadn't lowered the rolling pin, and the leprechaun looked between the two females like he couldn't decide who was the greater threat.

Getting a good look at his face for the first time, I trailed the sundry of freckles all over his light skin. His nose was slightly upturned, his eyes a bright forest green, and his hair reminiscent of the Gawama wild manes of curls.

"What is this about wishes?" I asked. I knew far too little about leprechauns. Any exposure I'd had to them came from studying a box of Lucky Charms while sifting through to pick out the marshmallows.

The leprechaun, whose head was beginning to drain of the excess blood, settled his face into what I'm sure he thought was a look of innocence. However, I didn't think the creature had a speck of innocence in him; he didn't pull it off—not even close.

"What do ya mean, wishes? What are ya talking about, lassie?"

Bab shook him a bit and he squeaked. "You brought up *wishes*. So tell Marla what she wants to know."

"Did I say that now? How very unusual of me. But then, I guess I shouldn't beat myself up too hard, especially not when it looks like ye are taking turns to do it for me. I've never been caught with me bollocks and sausage hanging out. 'Tis hard to think straight like this. I don't suppose ya'd put me down so we can talk about this like reasonable folk?"

"Tell Marla what you mean by wishes and then maybe I'll consider putting you down," Bab said. "But don't go thinking about making a run for it."

"And I want to know why you kidnapped me," Mindy added.

"Ah!" the leprechaun said with suspicious amounts of pep, gazing down at the hedgehog. "Yea, let's talk about that."

Bab looked at me.

"Mindy wants to know why he kidnapped her," I told her.

"Right," Bab said. "That too. You can't just go around breaking into pristine bakeries and kidnapping people—creatures, whatever."

"You also can't go stealing people's Spanx," I told him. "You've caused a lot of trouble. I've been searching for you all day like I had nothing better to do."

"Spanx? What's that?" he asked.

I waved my hand in the general direction of his attire, trying my hardest not to notice all the round buttocks and dangly bits he had on display. "Your shirt." I bent to remove the Spanx from where it remained pinned to Mindy's back. "And your knapsack." She stopped snarling and snapping while I made quick work of disconnecting her from Jadine's compression undergarment.

"Ah, that," he said. "Well, ya wouldn't go round blaming me none if ye'd had to wear obnoxious green suits for decades because ye fools imagined me dressed like a fooking happy-go-lucky eejit. With a hat and bright shiny black shoes ta boot. And the shoes be pointed! Do ya know how uncomfortable that is? The suits be itchy too. I hate them."

"What does the way you dress have to do with how people picture you?"

He stared at me for a long while, clearly deliberating how much he wanted to tell me. "People are stupid. They believe all sorts of lore without bothering to ask if it be true. Worse, then they start adding on, making shite up, and before ya know it, we leprechauns end up looking like dolls instead of powerful magical creatures."

When he noticed I was still waiting for a proper explanation, he continued: "What people believe of us affects us. We be very magical."

"How?" I asked, brow furrowed. That was some nuttiness ... if he was telling us the truth.

"Dunno. It's always been that way. So until all ya daft people start coming up with better ideas, ya can't go blaming me none for trying to dress better."

I arched my brows. "In women's underwear?"

"I didn't know these were knickers! How would I?

They be as big as a sheet, and they be black and shiny. They're also soft on my skin. No chafing here. Well, until this witch"—he paused to shoot a glare at Bab—"pulled me out of the sugar when I was fast asleep. Ya burnt me bits, ya know."

Bab grinned. "Good. You deserve it."

"And what about me?" Mindy pressed. "Why'd you take me against my will?"

"Because ya had that look about ya like ya be readying to shout up a storm. I didn't know they wouldn't hear ya none. I couldn't risk getting caught." He briefly struggled in Bab's hold, but the baker had too firm a grip, and his positioning offered him no good leverage. "Now I be fooking caught anyway."

"Karma," I said.

He scoffed. "Not bloody likely. I'm a leprechaun. Karma doesn't affect me."

"But people's imagination does?"

He glared at me, eyes flashing green.

Okay, then. Mental note not to antagonize the crazed-looking creature I still knew next to nothing about. Check.

Mindy, now free of the leprechaun's makeshift knapsack, turned to me. "Pick me up."

"What?" I said. She'd thrown a fit when I offered to pick her up earlier, right?

"Pick. Me. Up."

"Wow, way to order me around. Why do you want me to pick you up?"

"So I can give this creature and his flying bits a piece of my mind. *Please.*"

"You're in trouble now," I told the leprechaun, crouching down and offering Mindy the palm of my hand.

He eyed Mindy warily as the hedgehog scampered forward with purpose, tickling my skin with her tiny paws. She was cute as a button—if not for the vengeance scrawled all over her face.

I raised my hand so Mindy could face off directly with her kidnapper.

"You do *not* go around taking creatures against their will, do you understand me? That's a big no-no."

"Damn, I really wish I could understand her right now," Bab said. "She looks like she's tearing him a new one, all right."

I didn't bother interpreting for Bab. I didn't want to miss a word Mindy said. Besides, Bab was getting the gist, loud and clear.

"You say you don't like people's imagination affecting your life," Mindy went on. "You don't like something outside of you overpowering your will. Well, neither do I, mister. I am a *mother*. I am a *wife*. I am the *leader* of all the magical creatures who live in this village. I have big responsibilities to others. How do you think I felt not knowing why you'd kidnapped me or if you were going to hurt me? You stuffed me in a dark bag and bounced me around for ages. Then you locked me in a pantry, for crying out loud. I had no idea if I was ever going to make it back to my kids. And they need me, trust me. If I were to leave their rearing to my husband, they'd grow to be as foolish as you, walking around naked, draped in women's undergarments. You didn't even talk to me! You didn't tell me what was going on, no matter how many times I asked."

At least the leprechaun had the grace to look sheepish. "That's why I stuck me head in the sugar bin. I couldn't stand to hear ya shouting at me anymore."

"You could have just talked to me, you know."

"No, I didn't. And then I tasted the sugar. It was so good, I burrowed myself into it and fell asleep." He studied the hedgehog. "I didn't know ya be a mother and all. Me mum would skin me hide if she were alive and knew I took a mother from her bairns."

"And she'd be right for doing it too," Mindy said. "My kids would never do something like this. I've taught them better."

The leprechaun blanched. "Me mum taught me better too. This isn't her fault. It's mine. I've been alone for too long, methinks."

Mindy tilted her head upward. "Well. Then make

it right."

"How?"

"You can start by fixing your mistakes. Apologize and work to make things right with this baker woman. And then you'll have to do the same with Jadine. She's the woman whose undergarments you're wearing."

"I suppose I can do that."

"Of course you *can* do that. Question is, are you all bluster or do you really want to make your mom proud by fixing your mistakes?"

His little jaw clenched beneath a mop of wild, wavy orange hair. If not for the lighter tone, his hair looked a lot like Clyde's.

"Don't be giving me orders. You're not me ma."

"So it's all bluster, is it?"

He waggled his jaw some more. "I don't need ta explain myself to ye. Just go read the tales and make yer assumptions of me like everyone else does."

"I'm nothing like everyone else."

"Me neither," I interjected.

"Hmm," he said. "That would be nice. Though I'm still hanging here, arse out."

"Maybe we'll let you down if you answer our questions," I said.

"Or maybe not," Bab said.

"What's this about wishes?" I asked.

His eyes hardened. "Ye be just like everyone else.

They always be trying to catch me just so I'll grant them wishes. They don't care that I'm no genie. They treat me like one."

"Do you know what he's talking about?" I asked Bab.

"Not a clue. Sounds to me like he's just blowing hot air to distract us from his transgressions."

"I am not," the leprechaun said. "I can too grant three wishes to anyone who catches me."

He pursed his lips shut while heat crawled up his face.

"So I can make three wishes?" Bab asked.

He flared his nostrils but didn't say another word.

"How do I do it?"

"You're not supposed ta be able to make the wishes, 'cause nobody ever catches me. I'm fast and wily."

Bab snorted. "Unless you're taking a nosedive into my sugar."

The leprechaun looked away, staring at a wall of shelves lined with all sorts of baking accoutrements, all in perfect order.

Looking to Mindy and me, Bab shrugged. "Seems like I may as well give it a go. What should I wish for? I could use a new oven. One of them big stainless-steel industrial types would do me just fine."

"No, Bab," I said. "You can't. If this wish thing is real, you've got to use it for the town."

"He said I've got three since I caught him."

"Then use the first for the town, and the other two to spiffy up your shop or whatever you want to do. Remember that the council hasn't been able to figure out how to get Delise's magic out of the barrier spell."

When Bab hesitated, eyes all dreamy as she fantasized about an entire kitchen makeover, I added, "The barrier spell is the most important spell in the whole town. Without it, we aren't safe here. No one is. For our community to continue, we need the spell at a hundred percent. What Delise did isn't advancing anymore, but we have no idea what kind of harm it might be causing, nor if we'll actually be able to fix it without her cooperation. When I spoke to her about it last, she didn't even look like she knew how to undo what she'd done. What if we can't fix the spell and Delise's magic breaks it for good? The town will be over. We'll all be at the mercy of the outside world."

"And all the meanies out there," Mindy added, though Bab wouldn't be able to hear her comment.

I worried that Bab might have a selfish streak, but she put my worries to rest quickly.

"You're right," she said. "The safety of this town is everything. It's the one place where all us weirdos can be ourselves." She nodded, convinced. "The town comes first. My kitchen second."

"If you're gonna be making a wish," the leprechaun said, "ya can't expect me ta grant it up in the air and folded in half like I am."

"It's the only way it's gonna happen," Bab said. "You look like you'll run away the first chance you get."

"Who? Me?" A nervous laugh laden with guilt rolled through him, all but proving Bab's point.

"I wish—" Bab started, and I hurried to interrupt her.

"You're right in that he seems wily. Word your wish really carefully. Use all the legalese."

"Got it." Bab straightened her shoulders in determination, finally revealing signs of strain at holding the leprechaun up all this time. He probably only weighed thirty or forty pounds. Even so, I suspected my arm would have shaken right off by now. Bab's was only trembling slightly. But then, I didn't pound dough into submission all day long, every day of my life.

"Leprechaun," Bab said. "Wait. Maybe I should have his name. What's your name, leprechaun?"

"I'm not gonna tell ya that! Bad enough ya already have me strung up like a goose."

"Fine. *Leprechaun*, grant me my first wish." She took a deep, steadying breath and released it slowly. "I wish for the barrier spell that protects this town to be fully repaired."

"Tell her to specify that it's Gales Haven," Mindy directed urgently. "I don't trust him."

Agreeing, I relayed her directives.

Bab said, "Don't go granting my wish, leprechaun, till I tell you it's complete. I wish for the barrier spell that completely covers and protects all of the town we are in, which is called Gales Haven, to be completely and fully fixed. I wish for Delise Contonn's magic to be removed from it and whatever damage or changes she caused to be completely repaired. I also wish for the barrier spell to work as well as it was before she added her powers to it, and even better."

Bab looked to me, also flicking a glance at Mindy. "Should I also wish that the barrier become impenetrable? Like, so that the barrier spell can never be broken again?"

"Yes," I answered right away.

"Sounds risky," Mindy said. "What if that changes things in ways we can't anticipate right now?

I relayed Mindy's concerns to Bab, and then we all mulled it over thoughtfully, even the leprechaun.

"Seems ta me it's not right ta keep everyone else out," he commented. "I only got in 'cause I happened ta be in the area when the spell broke. My magic be so powerful, I only needed a little dip ta get in."

After deliberating for a moment, and well aware that there might be unanticipated cons to this plan, I told Bab, "Do it. Whatever happens will be better than having Delise's magic in there doing who knows what. Not even Everleigh has been able to reweave the barrier spell without Delise's magic getting in the way. And you know Everleigh is a badass."

"No doubt," Bab said. "We've got to do it." She faced the leprechaun again. "This is in addition to the terms of my wish as I've already stated them. I also wish that the barrier become resistant to any future interference or attack. The barrier spell will remove Delise Contonn's magic, reweave itself perfectly, including the provisions for Marla's daughter Macy being able to remain in Gales Haven while coming and going as she pleases, without any damage to the barrier spell."

That Bab would remember my daughter in the midst of all this chaos warmed my heart.

"My wish is to make the barrier spell so strong that no one can break it, and no one can come into the town ... without the unanimous approval of the entire council of Gales Haven."

"That's great, Bab," I interjected. "Awesome idea."

Encouraged, she continued, "My wish makes the barrier spell indestructible, and the only way any changes of any sort can be made to it is with the complete and unanimous permission of the entire Gales Haven Council."

Then she looked to me and Mindy. "Good

enough?"

I shrugged and grimaced. "I hope so. I can't think of anything else to add to your wish."

"Neither can I," Mindy said. "But I don't trust him. I don't trust anyone who would kidnap on a whim."

"Mindy doesn't trust him," I told Bab.

"Well neither do I," she said. "But if that's all we can think of, then, leprechaun, that completes my wish. Uh, fulfill it, or whatever I'm supposed to say."

"Treated like I'm a bloody genie," he grumbled in her hold. "Fine. Have yer wish already."

Blinding orange and green light flashed, filling the kitchen. Mindy and I squealed in shock, and Bab screamed.

With my eyes scrunched tightly shut, I waited, hoping the intensity of that blast hadn't seared my retinas, and that Bab was all right.

When I could finally see again, the first thing I did was check on Bab. She looked frazzled, her peppered hair standing on end as if she'd slipped her entire hand into an electric socket. Her breathing came fast, and her eyes were too wide, but she otherwise looked okay.

"That bugger," she snarled. "He gave me the slip."

Damn.

She was right. He was gone. And he'd taken Jadine's Spanx with him.

CHAPTER FOURTEEN

MINDY and I searched the prep area while Bab returned to man the counter out front, but there was no sign of the rapscallion anywhere. He'd either vanished, courtesy of his magic, or sprinted out the back door when none of us could see in the aftermath of the flash so bright that it had felt like an instrument of torture or interrogation.

Since it seemed that the leprechaun's visit to Bab's bakery was random, there was no reason to think he'd return. Mindy and I left soon thereafter. I offered the hedgehog a ride home, wherever she and her family lived, but she refused it. She said she needed the time to clear her head so that when she reached her kids she was once more unshakable.

I was beginning to admire Mindy. She was stalwart in her dedication to her family and to the magical creatures. I'd have to remind Nan of the hedgehog's desire to join the council as a representative of her kind. I was sure by now that the council members had seen enough of Mindy's devotion to the well-being of Gales Haven to vote to include her.

The fact that adding Mindy would rankle Delise Contonn to no end would just be a bonus.

Finally alone, and with more than an hour yet to go before Clyde and Macy got out of school, I should have gone back to Gawama Mama House to let Nan know what happened. She'd surely want to have Scotty check the spell to see whether or not the leprechaun had actually granted Bab's wish. The leprechaun could easily have been making the whole thing up; he definitely seemed to have a healthy dose of cunning in him. He'd been the one to mention the wishes in the first place. Sure, he'd behaved as if their mention had been a slip of the tongue, but it could have all been a ruse to secure his eventual escape.

I could have also headed to Bailey's New & Rare Books shop. Some research on leprechauns might help. But the little guy had claimed the lore about him and his kind was wrong. While living outside of Gales Haven I'd read enough books on supposed magic to understand that just because something appeared in a book didn't mean it was true. Besides, I was in no mood to spin my wheels. I'd been doing far too much of that lately.

I could have checked in with Wanda at her shop up the street, or given Jadine the bad news that it was unlikely I was going to recover her stolen Spanx—mostly because I was finished chasing leprechauns over something seemingly so trivial. Or I could have gone to Dixie's house to find out whether her locator spell had even worked in the first place. Was that faint sense that I wanted to check Bab's kitchen due to her spell, or had it been my own intuition humming along nicely as usual?

In the end, I didn't decide anything consciously, allowing my legs to lead me wherever they wanted. Clutching the bag of Enchanted Hearts Bab had given me before I left, I wandered along Magical Main Street until I discovered myself at the entrance to Moonshine Park.

Perfect.

Moonshine Park encompassed several blocks in the heart of uptown, nature sprawling in every direction, claiming this site as its own to be wild and free. The grass was thick underfoot, the trees old, large, and enchanting; benches dotted the landscape as the ideal escape from life's daily madness.

I claimed one of the benches, relaxing as I settled onto the warn slabs of wood heated by the early afternoon sun, breathing in the pure air that seemed nearly electrified it was so rich and alive. Placing the bag of Bab's goodies on my lap, I melted, releasing all the stress of the last several days as I stared up into the tree canopy overhead.

Quade had always loved it here. It was one of his favorite places in all of Gales Haven. When we'd dated, we'd shared countless hours sprawled across one of these park benches, letting the world pass us by, wrapped up in each other.

Tilting my face to the sunshine above, I allowed my eyes to drift closed as I enjoyed the calm of the setting. Like Quade, I loved the park, and I wondered how much of that was because he loved it. I'd run away, but he'd never left me despite the distance I placed between us. He'd always occupied a space in my heart.

"Marla," his voice whispered, and I briefly wondered whether it surged from my memories. My name was gentle on his lips, spoken with a reverence I'd never experienced from another man.

"Marla," he said again, and I decided it was real.

Opening my eyes, I smiled up at Quade in a daze. "Hey there," I said groggily.

"Mind if I join you?"

"Never."

He grinned like he used to when we were together, took the seat beside me on the bench, and after a moment's hesitation, also grabbed my hand, laying it on his thigh while he held it.

"Did the park let you know I was here?" I asked him, only partially joking. Quade had such a deep connection to nature, the premise was entirely possible. I hadn't seen it happen when we'd been together, but that had been almost two decades ago. A lot had changed since then—for both of us.

He chuckled softly, soothing to my soul almost as much as the rhythmic rustling of the leaves from the trees overhead. "No, I was here already. I was working with one of the oaks. She's old and usually so strong, but lately she's been struggling."

"Why?" I asked, more alert now. I realized how much the oaks from precolonial times meant to him. Gales Haven contained dozens of oaks that were hundreds of years old, and several of them were within the park's boundaries.

He rubbed a hand across the scratchy stubble on his cheeks. "I'm not sure."

He looked beautiful, the way the sunlight illuminated his whiskey-colored eyes and flashed across his dark long hair and easy smile.

"It's almost like she's ... sad," he went on. "I don't understand it. I don't know why she feels that way."

"Well, have you talked to her about it?" To anyone else the question would be odd. But Quade had already been talking to plants when I first met him in grade school.

"I've been trying, but she hasn't been talking back much. If she were a person, I'd say she's depressed. She isn't in the mood to do much of anything."

"Hmmm," I commented thoughtfully. The oak would be a large tree. I wasn't sure what they did beyond continuing to grow ever out and upward.

The silence drew out between us until I stopped wondering how I could help the tree; no one was better suited to discover a solution than Quade.

"Is this okay?" he finally asked.

"What?" I gazed over at him lazily, wondering if every afternoon could be like this.

He held up our joined hands. "I didn't ask first."

Smiling at him, I stared until I had my fill. The man was gorgeous, but that was as much due to all the goodness inside him that radiated out as to his objectively pleasant looks. If not for his personality, I didn't figure he'd be as much of a looker as he was. His kindness shone outward, in every one of his warm smiles, in every look of his compassionate eyes.

"I'm glad you want to hold my hand," I said, then prepared to apologize again for having essentially dumped him. But in the end I decided not to. We'd already had that talk, and I didn't want to continue living my life in the past.

Quade was giving us an opportunity at something new and precious.

Scooting closer to him, I leaned my head on his shoulder, nestling into him as I'd done so many times long before.

He sighed contentedly, making my heart flutter. We'd work things out between us. Nothing was ruined. Nothing was broken, not really.

As Nan said, I was transitioning into my perfect new beginning.

"I love it here in the park," I commented. "It feels like you."

He tilted his head down to look at me. "That's a nice thing to say. This is one of my favorite places in the entire world."

"It's true." I smiled. "What are some of your other favorite places?"

"In your arms."

I pulled back to search his gaze. He was serious and intent. His eyes blazed heatedly, like he wanted to make me his forever.

The smile dropped from my face as I met his stare with just as much intensity. The moments drew out while our surroundings faded into the background. All I saw was him.

I edged closer to him. The bag from Bab's bakery slid to the other side of the bench; our thighs pressed together through our pants.

"Marla," he said, whispering my name so close to my lips that they vibrated. "Will you go on a date with me?"

I giggled. "A date? Aren't we a bit...?" I'd been about to say, *Aren't we a bit old for dates*? Thankfully, I stopped myself before that nonsense had a chance to slip out. Instead, I said, "Yes. I'd love to go on a date with you, Quade. When and where?"

His smile was bright. "Tomorrow night? We can figure out the where later?"

"Deal." Grinning, I readjusted on the bench; the bag next to me crinkled. "Ooh, how about some of Bab's Enchanted Hearts for now?"

"Hell yeah."

His sweet tooth was as pervasive as mine. Between the two of us, we could probably polish off Bab's entire stock.

Dipping my hand into the bag, I told him of my plans to see Mo Ellen for an eat-all-you-want spell.

He grunted.

"What?" I asked.

"It's not because you don't like your body as it is, right?"

"No," I hedged, hoping it wasn't a flat-out lie. I mean, yes, I loved my body. But also, would I change this and that if I could do it in, say, a flash of magic? Of course I would!

"I love your body," he said, and my heart began thumping. "Don't change a thing about it."

"Well, quite a few things are different from the last time you saw me naked."

"Great. I can't wait to memorize your body all over again."

I froze, wondering if I could physically kick my own ass for having chosen Devin over Quade.

"Sorry," Quade said, misreading my thoughts. "Is that too fast? Do you want me to pretend I don't already know what you look like naked? Or that I don't want to make love with you?"

"Shit, no, Quade. I want all of that. All of it. All of you."

To cover up my sudden blush, I dug in the bag, crinkling loudly, handing him an Enchanted Heart and grabbing one for myself.

"Did you just sniff your Heart?" he asked.

"Hell yeah I did. Do you know how much I've missed Bab's sweets?" I groaned. "Oh my pickled pickle. Or Aunt Jowelle's cooking?" I smelled the Enchanted Heart again, taking my first bite. I moaned as I chewed, not caring that the sounds coming out of me could easily be confused with sexual pleasure. I didn't care. Bab's baked goods were seriously that good.

I closed my eyes to fully enjoy the deliciousness.

"I'd forgotten how freaking good these things are. I would've come back ages ago if I'd remembered."

I snapped my eyes open. Shit. Way to be insensitive. I hadn't come back for him, but I would have for a doughnut? *Good one, Marla.*

But Quade was smiling. "I'm going to pretend you didn't say that and focus on all the sounds you're making instead."

He leaned toward me. He was about to kiss me, and I could barely wait to feel him...

Then my Enchanted Heart was ripped from the hand I'd stretched out of the way to make room for Quade to get all up in my business.

I caught sight of a two-and-a-half-foot tall leprechaun running for all he was worth. The little dude was *fast*. By the time I jumped to my feet, all I caught was a final flash of his tiny little ass peeping out from under his black satin shirt, before he dove headfirst into thick bushes, taking my doughnut with him.

CHAPTER FIFTEEN

I DIDN'T THINK, I ran. I'd like to say that the theft of my doughnut didn't affect me, that I realized it was *only* a pastry, and that there was no need to overreact. I could always get more from Bab.

But my reaction was visceral. The sweet taste of maple glaze still coated my tongue, and *dammit*, I wanted more. That Enchanted Heart was *mine*.

I tore off at top speed, my car keys jingling in the pocket of my leggings, announcing my pursuit as effectively as the bell on a bicycle.

"Marla," Quade called after me before he must have realized it was pointless. I wasn't stopping until my hands wrapped around that little scoundrel's neck. His time of causing problems in my town was about to come to a swift end. I had better things to solve than mad capers all over town caused by a crazy little loon with his ass cheeks hanging out.

Before long, Quade's footfalls pounded behind mine.

I ran often. I'd been running since I was a teenager and discovered that the repetitive exercise soothed the busyness of my mind. But even though I'd been running a few times a week for decades, it didn't mean I was a lean, mean, sprinting machine. I ran a few leisurely miles, then rewarded myself with some pampering, usually in the form of chocolate, properly obliterating the effects of my exercising.

Quade caught up to me quickly, the extra length of his strides giving him an unfair advantage. Glancing over at him, he looked like a gazelle, or maybe a panther, all smooth lines and graceful movements.

I had no doubt my stride was far less graceful, but I was going to catch that bugger no matter what.

My intentions must have been plain on my face, because just as I was about to dive right through the bushes that had swallowed him whole, Quade grabbed my arm, pulling me up short.

"Wait," he said, and before I could object that the leprechaun bastard was surely using the time to get away, I understood what he intended to do.

This side of Moonshine Park was lined with thick, old-growth bushes. Their roots were deep, their branches thick and intertwined; their leaves made it difficult to see through them.

As if Quade were freaking Moses and he could part the seas, the wall of greenery started to condense to either side of where we stood, the bushes rustling loudly. Within half a minute, Quade's magic had carved a doorway for us to pass through.

And on the other side of it sat a leprechaun, his spindly bare legs crossed in front of him, the Spanx shirt blessedly hanging low enough to conceal his private bits, clutching my Enchanted Heart in his hand. I couldn't help but notice that my doughnut was missing several bites more than the one I'd taken.

"You!" I accused.

The leprechaun stared back at me, seemingly trying to decide how to react. I worried he'd run again, and even with my comfort with running, I still wasn't sure I'd catch him. He'd covered a lot of distance in a short time.

The tiny pain-in-my-ass must have decided the same thing. He leapt to his feet, shoved my doughnut in his mouth, clamping it with his teeth, and took off.

I lunged through the archway Quade had created and hit the patch of grass on the other side at a full-out run, not slowing down as I tore across a sidewalk. Good thing I believed in wearing comfortable, sensible shoes. I pinned my sights on the leprechaun's bare feet and chased them for all I was worth.

He might be fast and wily, but his legs were so much shorter than mine. Never before had I had a long-legged advantage in any situation. I was going to make the most of this first.

When I was only a few lengths from him, a tree he was passing whipped a limb out to snare him. The leprechaun whacked into the thick branches face-first with a loud *oomph*, sliding downward in their hold.

I slid to a stop next to him. The branches contained him in a band of wood that wasn't moving. The leprechaun had what remained of my doughnut smooshed against his face, his eyes dazed behind remnants of maple glaze and a delicious cream filling.

Certain he wasn't going anywhere, I looked up at Quade, who stood next to me, not even out of breath.

"Thanks for that," I said. "He's a sneaky one."

"Is he really a leprechaun?" Quade peered down at the little guy, who was a mess of pastry, orange hair, and shiny Spanx. "Everyone in town is talking about it."

"He says he is. He supposedly granted Bab a wish and fixed what your mom did to the barrier spell."

Quade yanked his head back in surprise. "Really?"

I shrugged. "It's what he said. But I don't trust him for a second. I've been chasing him around all day like I have nothing better to do than track his bare ass."

"Wha ... what is he wearing?"

"Jadine Lolly's Spanx."

"What?" Quade spluttered again. "Why?"

"According to him, he was tired of his attire and required an upgrade."

"Why'd he upgrade to Spanx of all things?"

"'Cause it's silky, shiny, and soft, ya big buffoon. Why do ya think?" the leprechaun said.

Quade smirked at him. "That doesn't mean you get to go around taking whatever you want."

"I always do what I want, don't ya know? Nobody cares about what I do now that me mum be gone from this earthly pasture."

"Well, I care what you do," I snapped. "I'm the one who's been cleaning up all your messes. And that"—I pointed—"is *my* doughnut."

"Is that what it be called?"

"Actually, it's called an Enchanted Heart," I replied before realizing I needn't explain a thing. He was a thief and a kidnapper. He hadn't earned any explanations.

"It be delicious, this Enchanted Heart."

Scowling, I debated what I should do with him. There was no point in demanding he hand over the doughnut, but what about the other things he'd done? Mindy, Jadine, and Bab wanted some sort of retribution.

I looked up at Quade, who was several inches taller than me. "I don't know what Nan wants me to do with him, but I figure she'll want me to bring him to her and the council. Will you help me?"

"Ya can't capture me," the leprechaun threatened. "I can slip any hold."

"Not this one," Quade said. "This tree has a firm grip on you. I can feel it."

The leprechaun narrowed green eyes at Quade until they became mere slits. Without interrupting his glare, he wiped the doughnut from his face, turned his ire on me, and licked what was left of the pastry off his hand.

"Mmm," he taunted. "It be *so* tasty."

I growled at him. Not because I wanted that doughnut anymore. I loved sweets all right, but that love obviously didn't control me. I wasn't even on my period, when comfort food became a necessity of survival. I narrowed my own eyes at him because I finally understood how Jadine felt about her Spanx. His actions felt like a violation of sorts, and he was rubbing that fact in.

"You can't do this kind of thing. Didn't your mom teach you any manners?"

He stilled mid-lick, apparently impacted by what I said, before continuing to lap up all remnants of his most recent crime. "'Course me ma taught me manners. She was always telling me what ta do."

"And now that she's passed on, you think *this* is the best way to honor her memory? By misbehaving at every turn? By harming others with your actions?"

He would no longer meet my waiting gaze.

"If you wanted to live here, you could have just asked."

"Nah, I couldn't have. Ye wouldn't have let me in, no ya wouldn't. That spell of yours doesn't let me kind in." He rose his eyes to meet mine, grinning. "Till that spell of yours finally fell. Bloody good thing I happened ta be in the area. I managed ta slip right in before it went back up, I did."

"You still could've asked," I said.

"So ye could treat me like I don't belong? Thank ye very much, but no thanks. Yer community here be exclusive. Ya don't let anyone in at all."

"We don't mean to be exclusive like you say," Quade interjected. "We keep others out only to protect ourselves from those who don't understand magic, and who would persecute us for who and how we are."

"Ya think I don't understand that?" the leprechaun asked. "I run and hide every day of me life 'cause of people trying ta catch me for bloody wishes or trying ta see if I'll ride a rainbow to some pot a gold or some other such fooking shite nonsense. Some folk actually think I can ride a rainbow! A rainbow. Do they not realize a rainbow isn't solid? They want me ta fall on me bloody arse from up high just ta find some treasure for them. Do they not give a thought ta me or me kind? Ya think yer persecuted ... try being a bloody leprechaun. There are so many legends about us that folk can't find the true ones any more than they can find their face with their arse."

"You should have come talk to us," I said. "We're reasonable people. We would've understood. I'm pretty sure the council would have invited you to join our community if you'd just asked before starting to steal and kidnap."

The leprechaun wiped hair encrusted with maple glaze from his face, leaving a smear of what looked like cream filling across his forehead. His freckles were concealed behind dirt and grime. "No one's ever reasonable with leprechauns. Do ya think people listened when me mum told them she couldn't find them a pot of gold? Do ya think they would've stopped harassing her afore they killed her from all the hassle?"

"I'm really sorry about whatever happened to

your mom," I said. "Really, I am. That sounds terrible. But now I have to take you to my grandma so she can decide what to do with you. She'll want to hear about these wishes too." I studied his wiry, small frame and the way he appeared smaller than before, wrapped as he was in the solid, thick branches. "Are the wishes real? Did you really help us with the barrier spell?"

He glared, the green in his eyes flaring.

"Well?" Quade pressed. "Are you going to answer the lady or not?"

"Not," the leprechaun snapped.

"Then I guess I'll have to make you."

A few moments passed during which nothing happened. Then the tree limbs that wrapped the little bugger started creaking, tightening their hold around him.

At first, he didn't do or say anything. But then the limbs kept squeezing.

His breathing grew shallow and his face red. "Fine, fooking fine."

The limbs stopped creaking.

I side-eyed Quade. His abilities had really progressed in the time I'd been away.

"I really did grant the wish the fooking nutter woman with the rolling pin made," he said. "But not 'cause I had a choice."

"So the wishes are real?" I asked, a bit of awe

tingeing my voice. I knew magic was real, of course I did. But leprechauns had been relegated to legend, even for us witches and wizards. It was like I was staring at a unicorn—albeit a very ornery, ill-tempered, runty one.

The leprechaun didn't answer, but his pout said it all.

I sighed. I was starting to feel a wee bit bad for the guy.

Spotting his Spanx knapsack flung off to the side, I walked toward it. "Come on," I told the leprechaun as I went. "Let's go talk to my nan. Maybe she can help you out. If you're nice about it and apologize, the council might just forgive you and let you live here with us."

I looked over my shoulder at him. "But you'd have to promise to be good and a helpful part of the community. There are no freeloaders here, and there are definitely no thieves or kidnappers."

Then I realized he wasn't looking at me. He was staring fixedly at his sack.

"What's in there?" I asked, though I was partly asking myself.

He opened his mouth—whether to answer me, warn me, or laugh at me, I didn't know, but by the time my self-preservation instinct started ringing through my mind, it was too late.

I reached for the bag, spotted something shiny inside it.

"Don't touch that!" But Quade's warning arrived too late.

Before stopping to think, I grabbed it.

CHAPTER SIXTEEN

IN MY HAND I clutched a dazzling, bejeweled blade. About the length of my forearm, it tapered to a sharp point. The early afternoon sunlight reflected off it, shooting prisms of light in every direction. A large, opal-like heart-shaped jewel sat in its hilt, drawing my eye like I was a magpie who'd found treasure.

My stomach fell. The blade's piercing edges weren't the problem, nor was its beauty. I was clutching a spelled artifact. I sensed the magic it contained vibrating through the handle, and whoever its true owner was, they were certainly a powerful witch or wizard.

One of the first lessons the children of Gales Haven were taught was to never, *ever*, touch an enchanted artifact when you didn't know what it did.

"Let it go slowly," Quade advised, obviously recognizing the nature of my predicament as I had.

I'd been bent over at the waist. Now I slowly squatted so I was directly next to the bag, and attempted to lower the blade back down into the sack. I set the blade against the interior of Jadine's Spanx, doing a fine job of not focusing on what had last been inside this particular compression garment.

But when I tried to gently unwrap my fingers from around the hilt, they wouldn't move.

"It won't let me put it down," I told Quade, working hard not to allow panic to infuse my voice. Freaking out wouldn't help a damn thing. Though maybe it would make the leprechaun happy. Had he allowed me to touch the artifact on purpose?

Swiveling my head slowly, like I was holding a ticking bomb instead of an inanimate knife, I pinned him in a glare. But the leprechaun didn't appear pleased or like he was waiting to gloat. He looked ... curious. I wasn't sure if that was good or bad.

Quade crouched next to me, placing a hand on my back. "Try again."

I did, and though I pulled with my fingers with all I had, it was as if they were super glued to the metal.

Shaking my head, I tried once more just in case. "Nothing."

"If ya lemme go, maybe I can help," the

leprechaun announced from where he still hung in the tree.

"Not a chance," Quade replied without even looking at him. "You've caused enough problems for one day."

"What if I promise not ta get inta any more trouble?"

"I don't think you're capable of that," I grumbled, staring fixedly at the sparkly knife I was holding against my will.

"Do you feel anything?" Quade asked, clearly referring to the artifact.

I sensed the magic pulsing like a heartbeat through the blade. I felt my own heart thundering, and the blood whooshing through my veins. Sweat prickled at the back of my neck, instantly making my scalp itch. My fingers twitched against the metal with the need to release the blasted thing.

"I don't know what it's supposed to do. I feel its magic, but nothing else. Maybe it won't do anything...?" I added hopefully. "Maybe it will let go of me if I just wait a bit."

Yeah, and leprechauns are saintly choir boys.

"Maybe," Quade said, but he didn't sound convinced of the possibility any more than I was.

The seconds beat by while I sensed the leprechaun's curious gaze on me like numbing pinpricks.

But nothing else happened.

Again, I attempted to release the blade. Again, it wouldn't let me.

Finally, I sank to the ground, folding my legs in front of me as I prepared to wait ... for what, I still didn't know. Whatever it was, hopefully it'd be over before it was time to pick up my kids from school. Sure they could ride the bus with this Gus who needed the job. But it was their first day of classes in a new town, in a new system of magic, and I intended to be there for them, whether they wanted me or not.

"Maybe if I just relax, the knife's magic will release me."

Hey, anything was possible, even if unlikely.

Quade just rubbed my back in reassurance.

More time beat by and the leprechaun ceased his squirming, apparently surrendering to the tree's hold.

"Anything?" Quade asked me.

"No. Maybe it won't do anythi—"

I froze, my eyes growing wide.

"What? What is it?" Quade asked.

"It—"

My view shifted. Quade and the leprechaun disappeared. Moonshine Park and Gales Haven vanished. Though I hadn't felt like I'd moved at all, and I could still feel Quade's hand on my back, clutching at me now, I was staring at an unfamiliar landscape.

Imposing mountains climbed upward, dusted in brilliant white. Heavy storm clouds dotted the sky, making the time seem later than it likely was. The air felt brisk, like I'd be experiencing a chill, but the temperature of my body didn't change, not even when wind whipped by, whistling as it went.

Where the hell was I?

"Marla," Quade said, concern apparent in that one word. "Talk to me. What's going on?"

"I-I don't know." Turning in the direction of his voice, I still couldn't see him. Instead, I made out a large field of wildflowers, bending almost flat to the ground with the intensity of the wind. "I can hear you, but I can't see you."

"What do you mean? Are you suddenly ... blind or something?"

I shook my head, but it made me dizzy, causing my surroundings to tilt and swirl. I stilled completely while working to make sense of the unfamiliar view.

"I'm fine. My eyes are okay. I can see, but I'm not seeing you anymore. I'm seeing ... someplace else. I have no idea where."

"Maybe ye're at the end of the rainbow everyone keeps trying ta make me find, the eejit fookers," the leprechaun said.

"What's it look like?" Quade asked.

"Just give me a minute to figure it out," I said.

The wind howled; a psychological shiver rolled through me. Carefully moving my vision as if I were turning my head, I continued past vast fields of flowers, dotting rolling hills that transitioned into towering mountains. And there, nestled amid them, was a cabin.

A warm glow shone from its windows. I set off toward it at once—though I didn't really move. I couldn't have. My body continued to sit on the ground beyond Moonshine Park.

Even so, I was on the move. Like I was in some sort of virtual reality, I was simultaneously experiencing two realities.

I crossed what must have been a quarter mile in that alternate reality until I reached the cabin. Up close, it was a beautiful log cabin that was as inviting as it was unexpected in this otherwise deserted landscape.

Peering through one of its windows, I gasped.

"What is it?" Quade asked.

I held up a hand to tell him to wait.

But then ... he wouldn't have seen it. In the reality he occupied, that hand was fused to the enchanted blade.

He'd have to figure it out. Because I just realized who occupied this peculiar charming cabin.

Irma Lamont was stretched out on a burgundy

leather armchair by a roaring fire, her legs propped up on a matching ottoman. She sipped at a cup of tea while conversing with two people who sat ramrod straight on a love seat: Delise and Maguire Contonn, looking as out of place on a *love* seat as any two people could be. Delise, still in her hideous pink poncho, alternated between glaring at Maguire and Irma. Maguire stared straight ahead without reaction.

Whatever had gone down between those two was bad—or maybe nothing at all had happened beyond apparently being whisked away to this isolation by a witch with an ability to zip-trip. Delise and Maguire had been married a long time, long enough for Delise's domineering attitude to cause long-lasting damage to whatever love might have once existed between them.

If not for its occupants, the cabin would have been idyllic, tucked away in this gorgeous scenery. The furniture was comfortable and overstuffed. The inside glowed with the flames flickering in the roaring fireplace. The place was quaint and other-wise lovely.

Before I could chicken out, I walked toward the front door and rapped on the wood.

From within, Irma's voice rang out. "Don't go anywhere." Then she laughed. "Never mind. You can't."

An eyeball peered at me through a saucer-sized window before the door swung open inward.

"Marla Gawama," Irma Lamont said. "I didn't expect to see you here."

"Trust me, neither did I."

Irma studied me intently. "How on earth did you find me? No one knows about this place."

"I don't know. I accidentally grabbed a spelled artifact and now here I am. Though I'm not really here, am I?"

Irma's lips pursed as she considered, then she reached out to touch me. Her hand slid right through my image. "No, I guess not. Either way, the heat is real, so come on in so it doesn't waste. It's chilly up here in the mountains."

Entering, it was even nicer than I'd imagined. I would have loved to vacation here. Well, except for the very angry woman shooting eye daggers at me from the love seat. Maguire turned to look at me, his gaze empathetic.

Irma closed the door behind me and took her seat again, gesturing toward another armchair across the room from her. Grateful to get off my feet, even if they weren't real, I claimed it right away. I was still feeling unsteady and slightly dizzy.

"Have you been looking for me?" Irma asked.

"Not me in particular, but yes, the council's been wondering where you are." I looked to the

Contonns. "And where they are. Half of them think you have Delise strung up by her toes like you said."

Irma laughed so hard her flat chest bounced up and down. She swept an errant strand of dark hair from her face, tucking it back behind her ear. "Trust me, the more time I spend with the woman, the more tempted I am. But no, I haven't done that—*yet*—though I am wondering if I should, just to avenge Maguire here. You wouldn't believe how she treats him."

"Oh I know. Remember, I used to date their son. I saw plenty I wish I hadn't."

"Right, I guess you would have." Irma retrieved her teacup from a side table and took a sip, studying me thoughtfully. "If people have been wondering where I am, let me guess. The artifact you have is a pretty knife."

My eyes widened. "Yes. How'd you know?"

"Because Dottie Hames has left that knife all around town. She's gotten forgetful, you know, over the years. She forgets where she leaves things. She had that knife spelled to help her find the things she's looking for. Only she always forgets where she leaves the knife. You'd think she would have chosen something a little less dangerous than a knife to have spelled. She could have chosen a teacup, for pickle's sake." She held her cup up. "But no, the silly woman has to spell a knife. She said it was pretty and she likes pretty things."

Irma shook her dark head as if Dottie Hames were in front of her and she were reprimanding her for her shortsightedness.

"So when I accidentally touched the knife, it brought me here," I mused. "Because we were wondering where you were."

"Exactly."

"And ... where are we?"

"Oh, it's a little place I had my sister create for me years ago, before she passed, you know."

No, I didn't, but I nodded in sympathy at her loss just the same.

"I figured I'd keep Delise here until she gave it up."

"Gave what up?" I asked.

Irma huffed, setting her teacup back in its saucer harder than necessary. It clinked loudly. "The way to remove her magic from the barrier spell, of course. We can't have that. The barrier spell is essential to our existence. Until she tells me how we're going to eject her from it, she gets to enjoy my lovely company."

Delise snarled and growled, looking feral in her dingy pink poncho.

Maguire scooted away from her on the love seat, which only allowed for a few inches between them.

"And Maguire?" I asked.

"Oh, apparently the crazy woman here has some sort of spell that links her lapdog to her. We were only here a few hours when Maguire just popped up. He's been here ever since. He can't leave her side. It's like an invisible rubber band binds them together. They even have to go to the bathroom together."

"You can't break the spell?" I asked.

"Unfortunately, no. It's not in my wheelhouse. I suspect Delise could, but she doesn't want to risk Maguire running away and never coming back."

"I'm going to kill you for this," Delise seethed.

Irma smiled at her, like Delise was a mental patient and Irma was enjoying the show. "Not if I kill you first." Irma cackled.

I shifted back in my seat, wanting to get away from all of them. Sure, Irma was looking out for the town, but her hatred for Delise felt real, and I worried the council member was letting it overcome her. Or maybe so much time alone with Delise had driven her to the edge and then over it. That, I could understand. Delise could drive just about anyone crazy given enough time.

I stood, wobbled, held on to an armrest and steadied. "Well, I'd better be getting back." Assuming I could get back. I had no idea how to make that happen. I could read the emotions of animals and talk to them. Not super helpful magic at the moment.

Oh! *Oh*. I totally forgot all about how I'd apparently absorbed some of the magic of Macy, Clyde, *and* Delise. How could I have forgotten?

But I did know how. I wasn't used to having all these powers. They didn't feel natural to me. And I hadn't had any need to use whatever I'd absorbed from the three of them. Delise could influence people's thoughts, so long as they were susceptible to her magic, and not everyone was. Macy could disrupt magic, and Clyde could link powers. I had to keep the scope of my arsenal in mind.

I finally noticed that all three of them were staring at me expectantly. Even Maguire's gaze had lost its daze while he took me in.

"How do I get back?" I asked Irma. "Do you know?"

"Not exactly. Every artifact is different, but I have seen enough of Dottie traipsing around town with that knife in her hand, looking for whatever she last lost to guess at it. I think whenever she finds what she's looking for, the knife releases its hold."

"Great. Makes sense," I said. "Though I'm holding the knife in Gales Haven, not here, wherever this really is." It hadn't escaped my notice that Irma hadn't actually told me.

"That I know of, Dottie doesn't ever leave Gales Haven," Irma said. "She always asks others to pick up things for her when they go. She probably has no idea the knife can help her find things beyond our borders."

"Okay. Soooo, I've found you. Let's return so I can get back into my ... body or whatever." I winced. I couldn't even feel or hear Quade anymore, and I guessed he was freaking out by now since I was clearly more here than there.

Irma shook her head. "Can't. Not until Delise spills the beans."

"No need," I said. "Her magic is gone from the barrier spell."

I hoped.

"How?" Irma asked as she walked her cup and saucer over to the sink.

"Uh, a leprechaun stole Jadine's Spanx, and then he kidnapped Mindy, and then he ended up in Bab's sugar bin. She caught him and he granted her one wish."

Irma turned to look over her shoulder while she scrubbed. "Seriously?"

"Strangely, yes."

"So it's safe to go back?"

"I think so. We haven't exactly confirmed it yet, but I'm pretty sure we're good to go."

Because the leprechaun had proven *so* reliable.

"All right, then. I must admit I'm pretty sick of the company. It will be good to get back to my little home and hand these two over to Bessie."

What Nan would do with them, I had no idea. But it was past time to get back home.

I walked toward the door, preparing to walk out it, though of course it wouldn't deliver me anywhere near Gales Haven. The circumstances were just so bizarre that I didn't know what else to do.

"You coming?" I asked Irma.

"Right away. I can take you with me if you want."

"Sure. I have no better idea how to get back to my body."

Irma led me over to her captives and asked them to link hands. When they didn't, she did it for them with sharp, snappy movements, mumbling as she went. "You'd think they'd be grateful for all the blessings Gales Haven grants them. But no, Delise, with her Napoleonic complex, has to go and try to ruin it all."

Without warning, Irma shoved her hand into Maguire's and claimed mine with the other.

In a whirl of green light, the cabin flashed out of sight.

Only then, I couldn't see anything. Not a single thing!

Blinking with mounting desperation into the pitch-black darkness that surrounded me on all sides, clinging to my skin, I cried out.

From very far away, I heard Quade answer.

CHAPTER SEVENTEEN

WITH A SICKENING WAVE OF NAUSEA, I pushed away mounting panic and forced myself to think—a feat none too easy when all I wanted to do was scream my lungs out and then switch to hyperventilating until I miraculously found my way back to my body.

Of course, a freak-out wasn't going to get me there. I'd survived enough to realize that sometimes I had to just suck it up and do what needed to be done no matter how I was feeling. I was used to pushing through discomfort to get shit accomplished. This would be no different, right?

Right.

I could do this. I especially could since I had no damn choice.

I could hear Quade calling for me. Now Quade

was as chill as they came, but he didn't sound calm. That must mean my body was still beside his, and it must appear to be an empty shell. No wonder he sounded like he was losing it. His words were a bit garbled, as if he were speaking to me from a great distance, but I picked up the gist of them. He was as desperate for me to return as I was.

The fact that I could hear him at all was encouraging. Theoretically, my consciousness wasn't in my body since it was hovering in a void of nothingness. But if I could hear him, it must mean that a part of my consciousness somehow remained with my physical form. And if there was a part of me that still remained there, I could find my way back. It had to be possible.

I figured when Dottie's artifact sent me to Irma's cabin to find what I was looking for, I ran into some serious glitches. From what Irma said, Dottie never used the blade beyond the boundaries of Gales Haven. I assumed the knife sent me so far beyond Gales Haven that it didn't know how to retrieve me. My consciousness hadn't exactly been transported to Los Angeles or New York City.

Irma was a Lamont. She came from a long line of powerful witches who'd been kicking ass since the town's founding. Her sister would have been one of them too. It was within the realm of possibilities that Irma's cabin was entirely magical and imaginary.

Meaning there was no map that pointed between the cabin and Gales Haven for the blade to follow.

So how was Dottie's artifact supposed to return me to Gales Haven if it struggled to find my location in the first place?

Most likely, my hand still gripped the blade, meaning I was still connected to the artifact's magic. If its purpose was to locate what I was looking for, then return me, I needed to help it find the path back. Pointing it in the right direction would deliver me to my body.

I hoped.

Each artifact was unique. Two objects could complete a similar task, and yet the spells directing their actions might be constructed of vastly different spells. It all depended on their creators and the finesse each person had in crafting them. What I had to do was either assist the blade in completing its purpose or find my own way back to my body.

I still didn't know how to do either of those, but at least now I had two ways to go about it. *Good*. This was better. I sucked in a few deep breaths, ignoring the bizarre sensation of breathing when I had no actual body. Of feeling like I existed beyond my mind when nothing around me supported that fact.

Living in a town filled with magic users, and being a part of the Gawama family, I'd experienced my fair share of odd and shocking experiences. This outranked all of them. I was going to need shit-tons of therapy after this. Or better yet, I was going to visit Mabel and load up on some serious amounts of Happy Times and act like this never happened.

Excellent. My plan was fully fleshing out. I'd get out of here, then pretend it never went down, and live on to enjoy another day.

Also, I was finished waiting for things with Quade to unfold naturally. If now that I was back in town I was going to maybe die or get stuck in limbo on a regular basis, then I was going to live like it really mattered—*every single day.* I hadn't really made love to a man since I left town nineteen years ago. Devin didn't count. As soon as I found the way back to my body, I was making up for lost time.

Properly motivated with promises of shmexy-ness and Happy Times, I focused on Quade's voice. The man had been a beacon leading me home since I first met him. Too bad it had taken me this long to identify all the stupid decisions I made to get in my own way.

Encouraged and distracted from the severity of my predicament, I forced myself to focus and got right to it. I didn't hinge on the fact that I still didn't have clarity as to what *it* was, but whatever. Details, shmetails.

I had to somehow latch on to my body and pull my consciousness back into it.

Since I couldn't feel my body other than a general sense that it existed, I listened for Quade's voice. His calls to me arrived less now that some time had passed, but I knew he'd never give up on me. No way would he give up on me now. He was probably still right next to my body, where I'd last seen him.

Or … if he thought he could help me somehow by leaving to do something or fetch someone, he might not be there anymore.

Crap! I couldn't see a thing. I had no idea what was really going on.

Panic rushed in. I shoved it violently away.

"Quade?" I called out without any idea whether his name carried sound. "Quade?" I spoke again, but it was entirely possible I only formed the word in my imagination.

"Quade!" I yelled soundlessly, straining my ears to pick up on his response, no matter how faint.

Nothing. The silence that enveloped me was thick and thin all at once. It weighed on me like a mountain. Swallowing a cry that slipped through without my permission, I called Quade's name again. When I listened for his response—for anyone's answer—I again heard nothing, not even the whooshing of my panicked pulse pounding through my head.

Another wave of nausea rolled through me like it was a tsunami and I was the shore it was about to devastate. A stupid, annoying leprechaun, who stole an artifact when he had little idea of its power, wouldn't be the end of me. I refused to be lost to limbo forever because a Spanx-wearing punk wanted to cause trouble in my town.

Hell. No.

That was not how I rolled. I had to get back to Gales Haven so I could kick his tiny bare ass into the next town over. They could deal with him there.

Pursing my imaginary lips in determination, I pushed away the fear that reached for me with sticky tentacles, trying to snare me in its net. If I succumbed, I'd never find my way out. I knew it just as I knew I couldn't delay in finding my way back.

I had to move now.

"Quade!" I shouted.

And this time he answered.

"Marla? Marla!"

I clasped on to the sense of his voice and refused to let go.

"Keep talking to me," I said, pushing the words through my mind, hoping he somehow heard them. "I need to follow your voice back."

The silence that arrived after my plea nearly broke my heart.

But then I heard him again.

"Come back to me. I waited for you for too long to lose you now."

How would I follow his voice home when I was a disembodied thought form? Without a better idea, I pictured myself in my body, reaching up to embrace him. First I threw that pretty blade so far away it would never bother anyone again, and *then* I reached up for Quade and kissed those amazing soft lips of his. Leprechaun be damned, I was slipping Quade the tongue, right in front of the pesky little bugger. Suffering through some PDA was the least of the punishments coming his way.

"I love you, Marla Gawama. Come back to me. Please."

Quade's words speared through whatever space separated us, lodging straight in my heart, making it beat like it was within my body.

For the first time since Irma zip-tripped away from her cabin and left my consciousness behind, I felt my heart beat within me—and I didn't think it was imagined.

"Keep going," I prompted, hoping for more of what he'd said, feeling like I could drown myself in his love like it was maple glaze. I'd float in it, swim in it buck naked, reveling in all this man and I would share.

"Your Aunt Jowelle just got here. She'll guide you back into your body."

But even though he said it like it was a done deal, I could sense his concern, his desperate hope. Was there any guarantee Aunt Jowelle could get me back? Probably not. But her abilities did lie with the mental body, and she was as fierce as any Gawama, even if she was tied up in hang-ups of her own.

"Luanne and Shawna are here too," Quade said. "We figured it couldn't hurt to have the trio work on bringing you back."

Good. Aunt Luanne rocked the emotional body and Aunt Shawna the spiritual. It'd be great if my mom were here to cover the physical body; then they could definitely bring me back. But I wouldn't waste energy wishing for something that would never happen. Neorah hadn't been here to save the day in a very long time.

"Your aunts have a plan," Quade was saying. "They'll get you back. They have to." His voice broke and my heart squeezed.

That was real. I definitely felt that.

I was almost back!

I could make it on my own.

Identifying the imaginary thread that linked me to my body, I yanked on it with all I had, pulling myself back next to Quade—when I felt Aunt Jowelle.

She was there with Aunt Shawna and Aunt Luanne, and with a strength of will that was entirely Gawama, they tugged on my consciousness so hard that vertigo swirled through me, making me feel sicker than ever before in my life, and fully disoriented.

Combined with my magic, theirs was too much.

I clenched my eyes shut, wishing the movement to stop. Wishing for steadiness and a body to ground me.

Strong arms circled around my upper body and I was suddenly pulled upward and pressed into Quade's chest. His heart beat out his desperation and relief beneath my ear.

Wrenching away, I tried to break free of his hold. He held me tighter against him, probably thinking he was keeping me in the here and now before I could disappear again.

I threw up all over his shirt.

CHAPTER EIGHTEEN

I SLAMMED my face back into Quade's now vomit-covered shirt, desperate for the spinning to stop. I breathed deeply until I sucked in the rancid scent of partially digested food, choking and coughing on the smell. Turning my head away, I leaned in Quade's hold until I hung off to the side, pressed against his upper arm, sucking in big swallows of fresh air. His bicep strained under the effort of holding up my weight at the awkward angle.

He rubbed his hand along my back in what was meant to be soothing circles. It worsened the spinning sensation. "No," I choked out, and he immediately stopped.

Aunt Shawna appeared in front of my unfocused gaze. Seconds later, Aunt Luanne popped up, crouching beside her. Aunt Jowelle and Nan stood behind both of them.

"Marla, my girl," Nan said, concern creasing her lined face, making her appear every one of her ninety-six years. "Are you all right, honey?"

"Mm. Mmm-hmm," I mumbled. It was all I had in me at the moment, though I regretted not saying more as soon as I saw my aunts and nan exchange worried looks.

I closed my eyes and waited for the swirling to stop.

After what seemed like a small eternity, the Tilt-A-Whirl ride inside my head came to a full stop and I almost cried out in relief. Everything was once more still, *blessedly* still. When I pulled back in Quade's hold, the vomit that coated his chest was cold.

Grimacing, I took in the extent of the damage. It was everywhere. All over him, all over me.

Reading my mind, he shook his head. Thankfully, his beautiful dark hair was unscathed.

"Don't think on it for a second, Marla," he said. "I'm so glad you're back. You had me so freaking worried. Don't you dare apologize."

Smiling weakly at him, I didn't apologize. It wasn't even the first time I'd puked all over him. When we were teenagers, we'd set off to get super drunk on Beebee's Monster Drunk Brew. We'd succeeded. I'd learned why the beer was given that moniker, and what exactly it meant to get "monster drunk." The result hadn't been pretty; most of it ended up all over Quade; the rest splattered all over the forest floor where we'd been tucked away behind Gawama Mama House.

"Are you all the way back? Are you feeling okay?" he asked, the deep concern in his voice proof he didn't care that he was coated in *yuck*.

"Mm. Think so."

He looked over my head at my family, eyebrows raised.

"I don't think she should move for a while," Nan said. "Not till we get her checked out and she feels better. She was really sick there."

Not moving for like an entire year sounded about right just then, but there was all the vomit. Quade might not mind it, but I sure did.

"Jo, fetch Willow, will ya?" Nan said.

After another worried glance at me, Aunt Jowelle walked away, leaving me wondering who the hell Willow was and what she could do to help. Was she some doctor? Because I doubted even a doctor in a village filled with the bizarre would be ready for what had happened to me.

"What's going on?"

At hearing Macy's voice, I forced myself to focus and take in the extent of my surroundings. Twenty or thirty townsfolk had gathered behind my family, all trying to get a look at me. We were still on the other side of Moonshine Park, where we'd trapped the leprechaun.

The little dude ... I wanted to strangle him! Just as soon as I could move, of course.

He should still be trapped in the tree behind me, but I couldn't turn to check, not just yet.

"What's happening?" Macy asked Nan as she slid into place beside her. Then she noticed me. "Mom? Mom! Nan, what's going on?"

My calm and collected daughter had accelerated to full-out panic in seconds.

"Shhh, honey," Nan said, patting her on the back. "She's gonna be all right."

I offered Macy a weak smile, hoping it would be reassuring, but it seemed to have the opposite effect. She spun to look behind her, frantic almost, making me wonder what the heck she was doing—until Clyde emerged from the crowd.

His eyes bulged with instant worry.

"I'm 'kay," I mumbled, trying to sit up. I managed it, wobbled, becoming instantly dizzy before leaning back into Quade, and into the puke that covered him.

"This is why the bus brought us here?" Clyde asked. "What the hell happened?"

"Yeah, what?" Macy parroted.

"Your mom touched a spelled artifact," Aunt

Shawna said, "and it yanked her out of her body. She's back now."

Eyes so wide I could make out the whites on all sides, Macy asked, "How long was she ... out of her body?"

"A couple of hours," Quade said, and I sucked in a sharp breath.

No wonder he'd been panicked!

"I found Willow," Aunt Jowelle called out as she and a young woman with rich chocolate skin and an awesome afro rushed over to us.

Willow knelt next to me, right in the slop of Aunt Jowelle's leftovers. I winced and went to try to warn her, but her smile was so warm and bright, I didn't bother, conserving my energy. She was mesmerizing.

Within moments, the yuck began dissolving. Her magic continued until it had completely vanished and Quade smelled as fresh as he always did, like a crisp forest.

My astonishment must have been apparent, because she smiled at me some more before saying, "My magic can clean anything."

"Wow, thank you. Will you come over to my house?" I laughed, all of a sudden realizing I was once more cogent and able to speak. And then I remembered I now lived in Gawama Mama House, which meant the cleaning wasn't all on me anymore, and the house mostly cleaned itself—courtesy once more of Great-Great Granny Jemima.

Willow laughed graciously just the same, surely as in the know of my new circumstances as the rest of the townsfolk. She squeezed my shoulder. "Glad I could help. It's not often my magic gets to be the center of attention."

Her energy was awesome; I instantly wanted to be her best friend. She turned and walked off into the growing crowd and disappeared without another word.

Clean and refreshed, and with the disorienting spin of vertigo over, I was ready to assure my family that I was feeling better.

Perhaps before I was fully ready for it, I disengaged from Quade and sat, hugging my knees and plastering a reassuring smile on my face.

Macy and Clyde grew more worried, their brows drawing lower, telling me I hadn't been convincing. They walked toward me, settling on the ground to either side of me.

"What happened?" Macy asked again.

I patted her hand. "I'll tell you all about it later—promise. First, I have a leprechaun to murder."

But when I turned—incredibly slowly—to find the little twerp with the Irish brogue, he was nowhere to be found. Carefully, I swiveled back around to face Quade, unwilling to upset my tenuous equilibrium despite my shock.

"Where is he?" I asked. While I was facing the other way, Harlow had appeared at her dad's side. She rested her hand on his shoulder in quiet support, sparking a pang of regret in me. To think Quade could have been my children's father instead of Devin. Of course, Macy and Clyde wouldn't have been the same, and I wouldn't change them for the world—well, maybe I'd tidy up some of their more annoying traits if given a fairy wand that preserved the rest of them. Still, knowing Quade would never be the father of my children was a hard pill to swallow. He was so much better at it, so much more loving and caring, than Devin could ever be.

"When your body went limp," Quade answered, "and I could tell you were ... gone, I lost my focus. I stopped communicating with the tree that held the guy." He shrugged. "The tree released him at some point. I don't know when. I was too worried about you."

"Dammit," I grumbled.

Quade shrugged again. "I don't care. We'll find him. I'm just glad you're back. It didn't look like you were coming back for a while there."

Quade vibrated with the intensity of what he'd suffered. Whatever tension I'd held on to released. He'd gone through hell and back too. Reaching for him, I took his hand and squeezed. He squeezed back, his eyes boring into mine, blazing with a need that only I could satisfy.

I couldn't believe I'd left him. I must have been out of my mind.

When I tried to stand, Macy and Clyde jumped up to help me, and a sharp reflection drew my attention.

The blade.

There it was. Abandoned on the ground behind me.

"Don't worry about that," Nan said. "Dottie's on her way to get it."

"Well, tell her not to let it out of her sight," I grumbled. "The thing almost killed me."

Though of course it hadn't. What it had almost done would have been much worse than death. Lost to a void without a body, without the ability to return...

I shivered, casting the thought from my mind. The worst hadn't happened. I was back. No need to suffer needlessly anymore. The ordeal was over.

Leaning heavily into my children, who were around my height now, I studied the crowd. Sure, what had happened to me would fuel the gossip train for days. But I saw more concern than greedy curiosity. The people of Gales Haven cared what happened to me. I'd traded the anonymity of a medium-sized city like so many across the world for a small town where everyone was invested in what happened to the members of its community.

I was really home.

"Did Irma come see you?" I asked Nan, aware that everyone was listening in on our conversation.

Nan nodded, though she still appeared shaken from what happened to me. "She found me to tell me you were supposed to come back with her but didn't. And then the big tree outside the kitchen at Gawama Mama House started knocking on the window until I came outside. It took a while, but I finally understood Quade's message."

Facing him, my brows rose into my hairline. "You can talk through the trees?"

"I didn't know I could, but I had to try something. I couldn't just sit here, helpless, watching the life leave your body."

I wanted to whisper kisses across his naked body, easing the pain still etched across his beautiful face. I wanted him to do the same to me.

"Come on, Mom," Macy said. "Let's get you home."

I was all for that, allowing her and Clyde to lead me toward the crowd, Quade and Harlow right behind us.

I paused by Nan. "Did Irma make it back okay? With Delise and Maguire? She has them both?"

Nan smiled a bit viciously, surprising me. "She has them both, all right. And Tessa just showed back up too. She's on guard duty at Town Hall, just itching to zap them if they try anything."

I sighed, relief settling into my bones along with a deep, overwhelming exhaustion. As if Nan read my mind, she said, "We can talk about everything else later. We've got it handled. Go get some rest."

"Yeah, sounds good." With the baton of problem solving passed, my eyelids drooped heavily.

Macy and Clyde started to lead me away, but not before I heard Nan.

"Quade, you'll stay with her, won't you?"

"Of course," he answered immediately.

"Go on into her bedroom," my pimping grandma added. "I've already told the house not to throw you out for breaking the not-married no hanky-panky rule."

I would have rolled my eyes, but I didn't have the energy. Numbly, I placed one foot in front of the other until a hand shot out to grab my arm.

I looked up into Wanda's big eyes. "Ohmygawd, Marla. Are you okay?"

"Mm-hmm." I offered her what I hoped was a reassuring smile, but was probably more like a twitch of the lips. It was all I had. "Fill ya in later, 'kay?"

"Of course, of course." She squeezed my arm before releasing it.

As my kids swept me out of the crowd and up the sidewalk—toward my car, I supposed—I heard Wanda asking my Nan what she could do to help.

Even as we put distance between us and the townspeople, stares followed us as we went. When we reached my car, Clyde fished the keys out of my pocket, tossed them to Macy, and tucked me into the passenger seat. Before Macy had even turned the car over, I was fast asleep.

Safe. Back in my body. Loved.

Home.

CHAPTER NINETEEN

I JOSTLED awake as Quade settled me onto my bed and turned to remove my shoes.

"Mmm," I murmured groggily, and he faced me.

"You're awake." He dropped my shoes to the floor and sat at my side on the bed. Leaning over me, he ran a tender hand through my hair, skimming its surface—probably because there was no way his fingers could run through it. Willow's magic had gotten me squeaky clean, but it hadn't performed miracles, which was what hair like mine required in order to be smooth and tangle free.

"How are you feeling now?" he asked.

"Better. Really tired. Crazy relieved."

"Yeah, me too. You have no idea how relieved I am. You really freaked me out."

I nodded in understanding, too exhausted to get

into it. I had no idea if I would have managed to return to my body if not for my aunts' intervention. Being outside of my body like that, trapped without a way back? Yeah, so not my wheelhouse.

Because of how dire the situation could have been, I wasn't going to focus too much on the what-ifs. They were scary as shit. The sooner I forgot about my unplanned field trip, courtesy of Dottie's blade, the better.

I made it back. That was all that mattered now.

That, and the hunk-o-man in my bedroom.

Staring into his eyes, visibly brimming with relief, I suddenly discovered myself far less tired.

"What?" he asked.

I smiled provocatively.

"Are you hurting?" he said.

So not that provocative...

I reached a lazy hand up to trace his upper arm, feeling the tense lines of his bicep beneath his shirt. Quade might be relieved, but tension still rode his body.

Speaking of riding his body...

He narrowed his eyes at me, the skin crinkling at the corners. "What are you thinking right now?"

"Why do you ask?" I said, again provocatively —maybe.

He studied me for a few beats, his gaze trailing my face and dipping across my collarbones, then farther down, skimming the swells of my ample breasts. Everywhere his attention went, it left tingles in its wake. My body was waking up.

"Because I'm wondering if you're thinking what I'm thinking," he finally said.

"I guess that all depends on what you're thinking."

"I'm thinking that Bessie told Gawama Mama House not to throw me out or otherwise interfere ... no matter what we do. Which means I don't need to worry about it throwing me out the window like it used to when we were dating."

I winced at the memories. Growing up, my bedroom had been on the ground floor, which was the only reason Quade had survived all the house's expulsions without severe injury. Though there had been that one time he got a concussion when the house threw him through the closed window, breaking the glass and all but cracking his skull wide open. From there on out, whenever Quade snuck in, we'd leave the windows fully open, even in the winter. The problem was that the Gawama women, particularly Aunt Jowelle, figured out what we were up to, and whatever hanky-panky we would have gotten up to without their interference was seriously curbed.

"Where is everyone?" I asked. "Where are my kids?"

"Once they were sure you were all right, I convinced them to go with Harlow to hang out at my house. I told them you needed the peace and quiet to rest."

"Why, how perfectly manipulative of you."

He shrugged with an adorable smile that made him look like the teenage boy I'd first fallen for.

"Does that mean Nan and my aunts are gone too?" I asked.

"Yep. They went straight to the town hall to deal with my mom and dad." At that, he drew back, withdrawing the hand that had been trailing across my bare collarbones and up along the side of my neck. His hands plopped heavily onto his lap.

I propped up onto an elbow and took one of them. "I'm sorry, Quade. I really am."

He shrugged in defeat. Though we hadn't dated in a long time, I understood some of what he felt. His relationship with his mother had always been turbulent, and I had no doubt he struggled with his father's meekness.

"It was a long time coming," he eventually said, visibly trying to shake off the burden of his parents' choices. "Here, lean on your pillows so you aren't straining yourself." He gathered my pillows beneath my back, helping me scoot up the bed to rest against them. So thoughtful.

When I'd been pregnant with Macy, I'd made

Devin go with me to a class that prepared us for labor. The teacher had demonstrated massage techniques to relieve the pain of contractions. Devin had somehow convinced me to practice on him—so he could learn properly—and I'd never once experienced the fruit of that class. He'd gotten a massage, and pregnant me hadn't. It was a perfect microcosmic example of how our marriage had gone. And of course, massage wouldn't have done a thing to help me during contractions anyway. Contractions were hell's dominatrix come to make us suffer.

Sighing loudly, Quade ran fingertips along my arm, returning me to the present with a quiver.

"I should probably go to the town hall to see what I can do to help," he said.

"Help who? Your parents or the town?"

"I don't know," he answered miserably. "My mom disowned me, did you hear?"

"I did. I'm really sorry." What else was there to say? Delise was a royal bitch who'd at the very least emotionally abused her husband and child. Thank goodness Quade was an only child. At least no one else had had to suffer through Delise's charms.

When I could tell I'd lost him to his worries again, I spoke to him softly. "Hey. You can go, you know? I'll be fine. You don't have to stay here with me."

"Bessie asked me to."

"Yeah, but that's only because, for whatever reason, my family's been trying to get me laid ever since I got here. I have no idea why. Do you remember how hard they used to work to keep us from sexing it up when we were dating?"

He barked out a laugh. "It was ridiculous."

I chuckled too. "Do you remember Aunt Jowelle? When she'd sit in the complete darkness in the living room or the hallway by my room, thinking we wouldn't notice her if she didn't move?"

"Or when she gave up on that and tried to use her magic to get into our heads to convince us that we didn't want to even kiss?"

I snorted—ladylike, that was me. "I couldn't figure out why I kept having thoughts about not wanting to have 'premarital sex' or wanting to remain 'chaste.' They were such Aunt Jowelle terms, but it took me forever to figure it out."

"We might've never figured it out if your Aunt Luanne hadn't put us on to her."

Chuckling again, I smiled broadly. "Aunt Luanne … can always count on her to encourage everyone to have sex. Her and Aunt Shawna. I'm pretty sure they'd be happy if the whole town had a massive orgy."

"They'd spearhead it. I've lost count of how many times I've heard them tell people that orgasms are the secret to longevity."

I face-palmed while shaking my head into my hand. "I have quite the family, don't I?"

"So do I. At least yours didn't try to stage a coup —or whatever my mom was thinking."

I looked at him seriously before busting out laughing, all vestiges of exhaustion fleeing. "True. Finally, after all this time, you've got me beat on outrageous families."

He shook his head, a few strands of his shiny dark hair sliding across his forehead, free of his usual low ponytail. Absently, he swiped them away. "Even after all my mom did, I'm still not sure my family wins the prize. Your grandmother and aunts have only gotten crazier while you were gone."

The mirth dropped from my face. "I missed them. A lot."

His eyes met mine, the whiskey color alight while he seemingly waited for me to say what he wanted to hear.

I knew exactly what he was waiting for.

"I missed you," I told him, and his gaze grew intense.

The seconds beat out to the rhythm of my pulse, speeding up the longer he looked at me like he wanted to claim me as his.

"Marla," he said softly. "I want to be with you again."

"Yeah, me too." I scanned his body, up and down.

"I don't mean making love."

"Shit, I do. After all this time, I want that. I really do. I want to make love with you." Like all the time. Every day, at least twice a day. Three times a day. Maybe at that rate we'll make up for all the time we'd lost, for all the passion we could have shared but didn't.

Chuckling, he squeezed my hand. "Yes, I want that too. But it's not what I meant. I mean, I want us to be together as in dating. I want to be your boyfriend again, or whatever term we'd used now that we're, you know."

"You'd better not say 'old.'"

"Hell no I wasn't about to say that. How about … 'seasoned?'"

"Seasoned to perfection? I'll take that."

"So? Will you let me take you out, wine and dine you?"

"Sure." I grinned like a fool. "Can we make out in Moonshine Park like we used to?"

At the mention of the park, I remembered the bag of Bab's Enchanted Hearts I'd left behind on the bench. Surely someone else had picked it up by now. I so didn't care.

Quade's smile grew to match mine. "Of course we can make out in the park. We can head up to Lily Lake and the Cracked Caves too."

I waggled my eyebrows at him. "And can we do all the things we used to do once we're there?"

"That and much more."

"*Much* more, huh? Sold."

"Awesome," he said.

"Super awesome."

We smiled and grinned at each other until my blood began to simmer.

"You're here," I started. "And Gawama Mama House isn't going to throw you out a window..."

He inched forward. "We do have lots to celebrate."

"Oh yeah? Like what?" I was flirting, proving to myself I still remembered how. I'd wondered if I'd forgotten after all that time married to the wrong person.

Quade leaned his head closer to mine until his strong chest pressed against my breasts. My nipples pinged to alertness. A shiver followed, running the course of my entire body, leaving me literally breathless with the anticipation of what I hoped like hell was about to come.

"I did lock the door to your room," he said. "No one can get in here unless the house helps them."

"And she won't."

"And she won't," he repeated, eyes beginning to glaze over from the heat building between us.

I tingled everywhere as he touched the tip of his nose to mine.

"I've waited a very long time for this," he said.

"Me too," I said, then smacked his lips in a quick kiss, unwilling to wait another moment for what I wanted with so much desperation.

His eyes widened in surprise, and he froze ... but only for a second. In the next, he returned my kiss and claimed my lips as completely as he ever had.

His lips were as full and soft as I remembered them, and when he urged me to part mine for him, I did, moaning when his hot tongue met mine.

His shoes dropped to the floor with a thud, and he shifted his body so that it pressed against the length of mine.

Hell to the yes. Come to mama. I was about to get some.

One hand swept all over my body, seemingly trying to touch me everywhere at once in a frenzy, while the other settled across one breast, squeezing it before sweeping the pad of his thumb over my erect nipple.

I moaned with abandon, surely sounding incredibly wanton, free in the fact that we were alone in the house that almost always contained too many curious family members. Aunt Luanne and Aunt Shawna would be proud.

With both hands, I gripped his ass, tugging him

against me, reveling in his hardness as it pressed against the money spot. He was already almost right where I wanted him. There were far too many layers of clothes in between.

Tugging his shirt up, he helped me pull it over his head. We popped a button as we went, but neither of us cared. The t-shirt underneath went next, and I hungrily ran my hands along his bare, muscled chest. He'd bulked out a bit since I'd last touched him. He was even stronger than before.

I, however, most definitely wasn't. I was rocking a post-baby mom bod.

When he slid my own sweater upward, I covered his hands with mine, stilling his progress.

"What is it?" he asked, gaze blazing hot so that I doubted we'd get to date at all before we made love. He appeared as hungry as I was to reconnect in that deep, intimate way. To reclaim the connection we'd both feared was lost forever.

"It's just ... I mean, you're amazing. Your body is as beautiful as before, if not more so."

"Thanks. So is yours."

I grimaced awkwardly. "Thanks for playing, but no, not really. Not at all, actually. My stomach and boobs have been stretched out so far they passed the point of no return. I carried around two humans and then I nursed them. You should've seen my boobs, leaking milk everywhere like they were a water balloon on its way to popping. And my stomach is Stretch Mark City. I even have a lovely C-section scar that pushes in, making my belly bulge out a little bit on either side of it. I now have one of those lower tummy bulges. Not really, but a tiny bit. It's not sexy at all."

I finally realized what I was saying and shut my trap. But the damage was done.

Quade pushed up onto his straightened forearms to perch over me, staring intently at me.

Wincing, I added, "Way to ruin the mood, huh? I never did learn when to shut up."

He shook his head at me, his ponytail tumbling forward over his shoulder. "That's really how you see yourself?"

"Kind of." And by kind of, I meant yes, absolutely. I'd come to terms with the fact that my body would never be the same, but looking in the mirror could still be painful when I studied all that my body had gone through to bear my kids. I was like a war survivor. I realized there was little I could do to change some aspects of my body. Sure, I could skip a doughnut or twenty, and I could run more often, but life was difficult enough without making it more so by denying myself the creature comforts.

I knew I shouldn't give a flying hoot. I wasn't just a body, I was so much more than that. And who cared if I had a whole zip code of stretch marks? I'd made *people*. That was like a superpower!

But Quade had last seen me naked when my body was pristine. It hadn't been stretched all to hell and back.

He pushed up my sweater.

"What are you doing?" I asked.

"Showing you how I see you."

Gingerly, he uncurled my fingers from where they clutched the hem of my sparkly purple sweater. Then he slid it up until it pooled beneath the bottom of my bra.

Oh crap.

I was wearing my utilitarian bra today. I hadn't expected to get any action. Bras for DD cups weren't the sexy, lacy things you saw perfectly displayed and color coded in lingerie stores. D-cup bras could only be found in the back of the shops, tucked away where no one would notice them unless they were the sops in need of them. They were big, cumbersome things focused on holding up twenty pounds of boob.

My thoughts and fears—ridiculous even to me, though it seemed I couldn't keep myself from having them—came to a swift halt when I felt the first of his tender kisses.

Quade kissed the center of my stomach, below my belly button, where the worst of the stretch marks squatted, unwelcome. He peppered gentle adoring kisses to the left, to the right, and lower, until he kissed a trail straight across my depressed C-section scar.

Mesmerized, a wave of raw emotion bubbled deep inside me. I couldn't tell if I was about to sob, scream, or laugh at how foolish I was to beat myself up the way I did. At how relieved I was to finally find myself back with this man again.

His love would accelerate my healing. If I could learn to see myself the way he saw me, I'd be set.

His kisses spoke of a total and complete adoration that tore through my soul, shaking my true self awake.

"Quade," I whispered.

Tilting his head up, he offered me a smile that warmed me in every single fiber of my being.

Emboldened, I pulled my sweater all the way off, throwing it to the floor with an abandon that shed a decade off me.

Tilting my hips upward until they met his, I said, "I want to feel you. All of you. Now."

His fiery whiskey gaze met mine, recognized my resolve and hunger. He pulled back, hands reaching for the button of his jeans.

Something plopped onto my cheek, bouncing off me and onto the floor.

I yelped, stunned. "What the...?"

Quade's eyes were as wide as mine must have been. He leaned over the bed and retrieved the missile, inspecting it.

"A ... piece of popcorn?" His face screwed up into a *what-the-ever-living-freak-is-going-on* look, one I also surely wore.

As one, we stared at the popcorn, then slowly tilted our faces up toward the ceiling.

"Ah, hehe, hey there," Hugh, whom I was definitely going to call Humphrey from now on since he hated the name, said to me.

"Humphrey," I growled.

"Is he talking to you?" Quade asked.

"Yeah, and he has a crap-ton of explaining to do, so give me a minute."

Hugh, AKA Humphrey forevermore, perched atop the single shelf that hung a foot down from the ceiling. It was currently empty except for the mouse who surely didn't belong there, especially since he held a small plastic cup filled with several pieces of popcorn.

"What do you think you're doing?" I asked Humphrey.

"Ah, em, well, I'm watching the show while eating popcorn. That's what you people do, right?" His face cracked into an *oh-shit* smile, making the little mouse look almost human—well, for a mouse.

"You're watching the *show*?" I asked, my voice growing deadly dangerous.

He laughed nervously. "Yeah. That's what I was doing. It was just starting to get good too."

I glared. Quade, seeming to understand the gist of what was going on, glared at the talking mouse too as he pushed to sit back onto his knees around my thighs.

"Don't mind me," Humphrey said. "I won't make another peep. You can keep going."

I stared until I was sure death rays were about to shoot from my eyes, cartoon style.

"I didn't mean for the popcorn to drop. I thought I had a good grip on it, but then things were really getting spicy, and well, I got a little overly excited, I guess, and it slipped."

I blinked at him as ferociously as I could manage.

"Seriously, you guys were doing well. Almost as good as those romances your Aunt Luanne likes to read."

Like a steam whistle, I bellowed, "Out! Get out now!"

He huffed. "Jeez. Fine. I'll go, but you don't need to be so rude about it."

"Me? *I'm* rude?"

"I'm glad you realize it. An apology would be welcome."

"Get up," I told Quade. "I have a mouse to flatten."

Quade climbed off me and I hopped onto my feet on the bed, stretching up toward the mouse.

He squeaked, dropped his sample-sized cup of popcorn, spilling it all over my bed, and scrambled across the shelf, squeezing himself through a crack in the corner of the wall and disappearing.

"He's lucky I'm short." I shook my fist at where the mouse had disappeared.

I breathed my frustration upward in a huff, floating errant strands of hair upward. I brought my hands to my hips and stood on my bed, waiting for thoughts of murdering Humphrey to pass.

Then I realized Quade was laughing. Spinning, I lost my balance, and fell to my butt on the bed.

Quade raced forward to try to catch me, but I'd already landed.

I pegged him in a squinty-eyed stare. "What's so funny?"

Shaking his head, his eyes watered as another belly laugh tumbled out of him. "There's never a dull moment with you, is there?" Then he laughed and laughed ... until I finally joined in.

When we were both wheezing and gasping for air, we plopped onto our backs on the bed, feet on the floor, chests bare except for my practical bra. We turned to face each other.

"So," I said, "want to pick up where we left off? Assuming we can forget that we had a mouse for a Peeping Tom. Like Tom and Jerry from the cartoons, only in reverse since Jerry was the mouse. I mean, he was really going to watch us … you know. With popcorn! Like some creepy voyeur at a peep show."

"Like I said, never a dull moment. But how about a rain check? When it's time, I don't want to be in a hurry. I want to go slow and enjoy every bit of you. Fully. Intensely. For hours. *Days.*"

I swallowed, nodding my eager encouragement. "I'm sure I can clear my mad caper detective schedule for that," I said in a husky squeak that sounded like I'd stepped on a dog's toy.

He ran a slow, sensual finger across my lips, down my neck, across my collarbones, and paused at the swell of my breasts. "Good. Because I'm going to start making plans for you. And I won't let you leave this time."

"Trust me, I'm not going anywhere. I'm home now. Here. With you."

He stared at me until he must have seen proof that I meant what I said. Then he nodded. "Good. Glad to hear it." Then he sighed loudly. "Ready to go deal with my crazy mom before she gives Tessa reason to zap her senseless?"

"As ready as I'll ever be."

When Quade and I emerged from Gawama Mama House, our hands were entwined.

Despite all the recent craziness, my heart beat a steady rhythm of happiness and the promise of all the wonderful things to come.

CHAPTER TWENTY

THE CONTENTMENT that fluttered inside me, beating against my rib cage, flew away like an escaping bird the moment Quade opened the door to the town hall for me. In rushed chaos and commotion, devouring the afterglow of our kissing.

Quade's hand settled against the small of my back as he led me through a crowd of standing townspeople and up the crowded aisle.

It looked like everyone in Gales Haven had assembled to see what the council would do with Delise and Maguire. Like any good small town, news traveled wickedly fast. Every single seat was occupied. The proceedings were standing room only.

"Are our kids here?" I asked Quade over my shoulder.

"I haven't seen them yet. I hope they're at home.

I'd rather Harlow not see whatever's about to happen."

I didn't blame him. The townsfolk, ordinarily peaceful enough despite their wild ways, demanded punishment for Delise's violation of their trust. I could hear it in the anger of their barely contained whispers, the way they shot nasty looks up at Quade's parents, who stood next to each other up front, facing the council members atop the dais. Nan, Darnell Adams, Irma Lamont, Stella Egerton, and Tessa Smate sat straight in their high-backed wooden carved chairs, representing the G.A.L.E.S. in Gales Haven as their ancestors had done. They sat in the same chairs, resolved to protect all that the village represented since 1803.

Knowing my aunts would be stationed near their mother, I easily found them occupying the front pew, their red heads standing out from their neighbors. I headed directly for them even though there was no space next to them. I had to find out what was going on and make sure they knew that the leprechaun had maybe—possibly—fixed the problem with the barrier spell before they strung Delise up in front of everyone. She probably deserved it, but I at least needed to make sure they had all the facts before they doled out verdicts. I hadn't managed to update them before I touched Dottie's blade and was transported away.

Reaching Aunt Jowelle, I crouched down so as not to obstruct anyone's view of the proceedings and whispered to her. "Does Nan know—?"

"Marla," Nan called out, and a hush swept across the Haveners. "I'd like you and Quade to come up here please."

I straightened, plastered a smile on my face, and marched up front. I'd only been in town for a few days and already I'd been summoned several times. The universe had thumbed its nose at my desire for ease and grace as I rejoined this community. I'd jumped straight into the proverbial frying pan. Quade slowed as he passed his parents. Maguire offered him a sad smile as befitted a man who was obviously utterly defeated. Delise, however, didn't deign to acknowledge her disowned son. She pointed her nose several degrees farther in the air. Given that she was already haughty, she now had to look down to see the council.

Quade sighed sadly at my side as we drew up to Nan.

Before she could say anything, I told her, "The barrier spell might be fixed. The Delise problem might already be solved."

She looked between me and Delise. When she focused on the woman in her now-dingy pink poncho, she narrowed her eyes dangerously. "No thanks to that woman."

"No," I said. "Possibly thanks to a trouble-causing leprechaun."

I expected Nan and the rest of the council to regard me curiously at that. It wasn't every day that people mentioned leprechauns—not even in Gales Haven.

But the council members continued to glare at Delise—at times also at Maguire. Nan just *hmmphed*.

"Bab told you, then?" I asked.

"Yup." She popped her P, not letting up the vicious stare she pinned on Delise.

The effect of Delise's returned glare was lost since her head was tilted so far back. The woman probably thought she was being regal. With her unkempt hair, sour expression, and wildly furious eyes, she succeeded only in looking deranged.

"And did Scotty check the barrier spell?" I asked. "Did the leprechaun actually fix it?"

"He did."

Relief whooshed through me. I'd broken the spell, and I'd felt the responsibility of fixing it until this very moment.

Sure, *I* hadn't actually broken the thing; my kids had. But what my kids did, I was responsible for. And though we'd repaired it and it had been broken again, this time not due to our magic, I couldn't help but feel like it was still on me to fix it. If not for me,

Delise wouldn't have been standing there at the barrier, hooking her magic into it.

Now, it was finally over. I could move on to other things. Hopefully tasks that didn't involve Spanx or tiny bubble-butted leprechauns.

Nan spoke so that only the council, Quade, and I could hear: "I fully trust Bab. No one can make Enchanted Hearts and Twisted Turtles that taste as good as hers and be untrustworthy. But since I represent a whole lot of people, I need to go through the processes and all that rigamaroo to show that I'm fair and impartial and all that. The rest of the council too."

I nodded, unsure what she was getting at.

"Bab told us that a leprechaun snuck into town when the barrier was down and then started stealing stuff. She says he took all of Jadine Lolly's Spanx so he could wear them as shirts because he was all nekked underneath. She says he kidnapped the talking hedgehog too."

Her eyebrows raised in question.

"Close enough," I said, registering how crazy it all sounded, how crazy my life had become. And even so, it was better than my life in the city with Devin. What did that say about Devin? And even more pointedly, what did that say about me?

"Bab also says that when she caught the leprechaun passed out in her sugar store, she yanked him out, gave his privates a bad case of the burn, and hung him upside down till he let slip he could grant three wishes."

I nodded, inappropriate giggles bubbling up inside me, which I struggled to contain. It was all so ludicrous! But thousands of curious eyes watched me, reminding me how serious the matter was, and what was at stake.

"You told her to wish the barrier spell fixed—"

"That was a very fine idea, Marla," Darnell interjected.

"Fine indeed," Nan said. "You saved our putuckuses, because Delise here is so spiteful I don't think she ever would've fixed it."

"I'm so glad it worked," I said, totally earnest. If it hadn't, I didn't know how we would have gotten it fixed. Delise's stance was about as cooperative as a stubborn mule's.

"Us too," Stella chimed in.

Nan nodded. "Bab was pissed the leprechaun slipped her before she could get her last two wishes. Said she could've gotten a whole new kitchen. The scoundrels are notoriously hard to catch."

"All but impossible," Stella said. "If you hadn't found him passed out in Bab's sugar, there's no way you would've managed it."

"Makes sense," I said. "He was a fast little bugger, and sly too. I still need to find him."

Nan waved her hand. "Don't worry, I'm sure you'll figure out where he is soon."

Yeah, and that's what worried me. What was he planning on stealing next? Someone's dentures? Another set of oversized underwear? Worse, another magical artifact just waiting to zap the crap out of some unsuspecting sod, AKA me? I swallowed an eye roll and a groan at the thought of what was coming next.

"Maybe you should check at the end of the rainbow," Stella suggested. "I've heard that's where you find them."

I winced at the memory of how belligerent the leprechaun got at the mention of that theory. "I don't think that's how it really works."

"Hmm. Good to know." Stella flapped her arms a couple of times for no apparent reason and then seemed to descend into deep thought. "Won't be doing that anymore, then," she finally mumbled.

A giggle almost slipped out until I turned it into what passed for a feminine burp. I brought a modest hand to my mouth. "Excuse me."

Nan asked, "So you confirm Bab's story is accurate? Delise here didn't do a thing to help fix the barrier spell? If it were up to her, her magic would still be hooked into it?"

"What Bab said is correct," I told them.

"If not for you," Irma added, "we might not have realized what Delise was doing until it was too late."

"True," Stella said with a theatrical wave of a hand. "Marla's saved our butts a few times already and she's only just come back. Scotty says the spell is stronger than before now."

It was kind of them to leave out the part about all the trouble I'd unintentionally caused. And who was I to remind them of it?

Nan looked so insistently into my eyes, I wondered what she was searching for. Eventually, she asked, "Anything else you need to tell us?"

"Well..." I suddenly felt like this was an interrogation, like I had to come clean before I missed my chance. But about what? How many times the blasted leprechaun had given me the slip? Or how ridiculous I'd felt running all over town looking for stolen Spanx?

"There are tons of little details I left out," I said, "but I can't think of anything else important there is to tell you."

"Okay, good," Nan said. "Then we can move on. We'll talk about your detective duties later."

Clearly dismissed, I stepped to the side, wondering whether I could sit down so everybody would stop staring at me.

"Quade." Nan beckoned him forward. He took my place, drawing the bulk of the attention to him.

"Because you're a respected member of this community, we the council would like to see if you have any input on what should happen to your parents."

Evidently startled, Quade snapped a glance at his parents. Only Maguire met his look. The man's hair was greasy and stuck to his scalp. His skin was sallow and his eyes sunken. Though Irma hadn't been gone with them long, the man was clearly broken. Of all the damage Delise had done, both to the town and her family, it pained me most to see what she'd done to her husband. She'd taken everything from him and denied him any chance at happiness. She was even trying to take away his son.

"You mean what kind of punishment I think they should receive?" Quade asked, lowering his voice to a whisper, probably hoping his parents wouldn't hear him discussing their fate.

Tessa leaned forward onto her elbows, looking down the table at him. "That, and if there's any reason to offer them leniency."

Tessa looked like her usual collected self. Everything must have gone well for her on her exploratory trip outside of town.

Tessa followed up: "Is there anything you know that we don't that will affect our decision?"

Quade considered his parents, running a hand along his long hair, squeezing his ponytail at the nape of his neck at the end—a nervous tell of his.

His mother grimaced, as if she couldn't stand his long hair even now, when her fate was being determined. She might have disowned him, but she hadn't stopped judging him.

Quade noticed, a deep sadness clouding those bright eyes I so loved. His back bowed slightly as he moved on to consider his father. Maguire met his son's searching gaze, his eyes shiny with tears.

"Stand strong, Maguire," Delise snapped, surprising me. I hadn't thought she could even see her husband with the way her haughtiness was on display. "Crying isn't for men." She smirked. "Or is that the problem?"

Her implication that her husband of decades wasn't a man rang clear as a bell.

Quade's demeanor hardened and he faced the council. "I think you know what you need to. There's nothing more I can add. And if you'll excuse me from the burden, I'd rather not be responsible for what happens to them."

Nan slid a hand across the old wooden table to take his, clutching it for a few seconds before letting go. "You aren't responsible, Quade, not for a second. You're your own person. Whatever befalls your mother and father is thanks to their actions, not yours."

"May I be dismissed?" he asked, tension rolling through tight shoulders.

"Yes. Yes, of course. Thank you, Quade."

Quade took my hand and led me toward the far wall, where we stood slightly away from it all, as if that physical distance could separate him from the fact that his family was being ripped apart.

Tessa Smate stood and the hall quieted. She must have been the council foreperson that day. "We have all the information we need to determine the punishment of Delise Contonn and Maguire Contonn. Hold tight for a bit please while the council confers."

The townsfolk waited, but they were far from silent as gossip billowed like a wildfire, guesses were offered as to the Contonns' final punishment, and bets were made.

Quade noticed too. "Really, Gus? You're gonna bet on what happens to my parents?" he called up a few rows.

Gus nodded enthusiastically. "You want in?"

"No I don't want in," Quade grumbled miserably, leaning against the wall.

He closed his eyes. I edged closer to him.

There wasn't much I could do to help now, but I could offer him my silent support. Unwavering at his side, I waited with him until Tessa stood once more to announce the verdict.

CHAPTER TWENTY-ONE

THE HUSH that followed Tessa Smate's pronounce-ment drew out. Never in the history of Gales Haven had any of its residents been permanently banished, but exile was precisely the verdict the council had just handed down.

"You can't do that," Delise Contonn protested, hands on hips, making her poncho flare out in an ugly pink rhomboid. "As residents of Gales Haven, we're guaranteed its protection. That's the whole point of living here. You think I would have stayed here all this time if not? Living with the likes of you, so ready to believe the worst of me?"

Maguire didn't say a word, his head tilted down-ward in evident regret. I assumed he was lamenting ever meeting the woman who stood at his side in the physical sense only.

Nan jumped to her feet faster than I thought possible, leaning her weight on her hands on the tabletop as she leaned forward to glare. Righteous anger was obviously fueling her actions now. "Of course we can exile you," she snapped, power riding her words as if she were decades younger. "By living within its borders, every resident of Gales Haven agrees to be ruled by the council. We do our best not to be invasive and to let Haveners live their lives as they please. I think you'd all agree we do a good job of not sticking our noses in your business."

She paused, looking out over the crowd. Nods and murmurs of assent rolled across the townsfolk.

"See?" Nan told Delise. "You endangered our very way of life. You threatened the security of three-thousand and sixty-nine people just because of your greedy ambition. You are being exiled because of *your* actions, your bad choices. No one else's. You have no one to blame but yourself."

"I blame all of you," Delise said right away, vehemence on full display. "You didn't see what was right in front of your faces."

"Clearly," Irma Lamont sneered.

Delise ignored her, a single twitch of the eye the only evidence that she'd heard Irma.

"The power of the barrier was waning. I told you that. I'm as powerful as any of you. You need me to bolster the barrier. That's what I was trying to show you. I was only trying to help."

"Help?" Stella repeated, incredulous. Like Nan, she rose to her feet, where her arms began to gesture theatrically as was her way. "You really expect us to believe you were only trying to *help*?" The more worked up she got, the more her arms moved, the loose flesh of her triceps wobbling visibly beneath her shirt. "You tagged the barrier spell, the oldest and most important spell of our entire town, with your own magic. Magic that was interfering with the barrier spell and causing harm. You didn't even know how to remove your magic! What kind of idiots do you think we are? You had no intention of removing your magic. You were going to coerce us into doing your will. And *that* is not the kind of behavior that will be tolerated from any of our residents. Luckily, no one else is so full of themselves as to put their megalomaniacal desires above the well-being of everyone else in our great town."

Stella, who had a taste for party wear even when it was gaudy, loud, and out of place, was wearing all black for the first time possibly ever to mark the severity of the situation. The muted black sequins of her knee-length dress dully reflected the vivid colors of sunset outside the large windows.

"Like Bessie said," Stella continued, "you have no one to blame but yourself. Poor Maguire just got caught in the web of your schemes, as usual. He's going to pay the price of your actions. But you ... you're paying for what *you* did. So be a woman about it. Own up to it and stop pointing fingers."

I'd never seen Stella like this. She had a slight wattle and it shook slightly with her fury.

Delise glared at Stella. The councilwoman plopped her hands onto the tabletop and leaned so far over it to do her own glaring that I worried her hands would slip out from under her.

Tension crackled in the air.

Softly, Maguire asked, "Where are we to go?"

Nan shook her head at him in commiseration. A few strands of her crimson hair tumbled from her chignon. "I'm sorry, Maguire, I really am, but that's on you. Once you step foot outside of the barrier, you won't be able to count on any of our aid."

"I understand." He didn't meet Nan's waiting stare, though her eyes welled with compassion for his predicament.

"I'm gonna give you some advice though you didn't ask for it. If I were you, I'd distance myself from your wife. Permanently. She doesn't look out for you. She's only going to lead you astray like she did here."

"I can't be free of her," he mumbled.

"Excuse me? Repeat that." Nan cupped a hand to her ear like she was hard of hearing. Only I knew that was far from the case. She wanted people in the back to hear him.

"I can't be free of her," he repeated, more loudly.

"And why is that?"

Nan had to know already. Surely Irma Lamont had told her.

"Because she has a spell in place that links me to her. That's why I ended up with her and Irma when Irma took her."

"*Her*?" Delise growled. "You're talking about me like I'm not standing right next to you. Bessie's playing you like you're some circus clown. Do you want to be a circus clown, Maguire? Huh, do you?"

If the choice were between being a circus clown or being her husband, I knew what I'd choose.

Maguire stared ahead only at Nan and the rest of the council, for once ignoring his wife. "Where she goes, I go. Whatever she wants me to do, she eventually gets."

Nan sighed somberly. "Yes, and that's why we are forced to banish you along with her. However..." Nan narrowed her eyes at Delise. "We might be able to break the spell that links you to her. My great-granddaughter Macy's magic could possibly do it. Then we might"—Nan looked to the other council members, who nodded their agreement—"allow you to stay on a probationary basis."

Maguire stared at his wife, who glared back at him, her hostility undisguised.

"Don't you dare, Maguire. I will never forgive you."

Finally, he sighed. "Thank you, Bessie, and the rest of the council members too. I appreciate the offer. But this is something I need to resolve on my own. It's been a long time coming."

If I were Maguire, I would have taken Nan up on her offer in two seconds flat. But then, I wasn't Maguire.

"If you're sure," Nan eventually said, "then that's your choice. But know that if some ill should befall Delise and she were to, say, die, you would be welcome to come back here."

Delise drew in a theatrical gasp, bringing a hand to her chest in feigned affront. I was starting to think the woman wasn't capable of real emotion. "Are you telling *my husband* to kill his wife? Me?"

"No. I'm saying what goes around comes around, and you might just find yourself on the butt end of some fearsome karma."

"Hmph," Delise grunted.

Nan ignored her, continuing to speak to Maguire. "Now, if you were to come back once Delise isn't in the picture, we wouldn't be able to automatically allow you to rejoin our community. You've made a lot of bad decisions over the years, even if I assume all of them were thanks to Delise. But we'd at least give you a chance, and we'd decide based on your actions alone for once and not hers."

Nan took in the rest of the council members, their expressions equally regretful, before facing him again. "We really are sorry for how it's turning out. But we can't chance allowing you to stay in Gales Haven when she controls you. We wish it weren't so, but let's be real, it is. So long as that's in any way the case, you aren't welcome here."

Maguire nodded in defeat, but didn't protest.

Then Tessa stood, looking out at the sea of faces. "If there's nothing more…"

"Of course there's more," Delise interrupted. "You can't do this. I was only trying to help. I did what I did to *help* the town when y'all were too dense to figure out you needed me."

Tessa sighed, but when Stella opened her mouth, no doubt to give Delise another piece of her mind, she stilled her with an upraised hand.

"Delise Contonn," Tessa said, "your sentencing is complete. We the council feel we have a clear picture of who you are and what your true intentions are. Even if what you're saying is truthful to your mind, and you genuinely believe you were trying to help, you can't be trusted. You endangered the security of the town without a single thought to the consequences of your actions. We have no guarantee you won't do it again."

"Especially not with your current attitude," Stella bit in, unable to help herself.

"Right," Tessa said.

"Just be glad we aren't stringing you up by your toes," Irma said. "That's what I voted to do."

"And I seconded it," Stella added, though I doubted either of the women really meant it.

But then, taking into account the fierce tilt of their eyes and mouths, it was hard to tell. Having been around Nan much of my life, I understood how seriously the council took its responsibility to keep the townspeople safe. It was their number one priority. Since Delise had proven herself a threat to general well-being, I wasn't surprised they were throwing her out.

Tessa looked down the line at her fellow council members, ending at Nan, who nodded. Tessa glanced at Noreen Bradley, who sat in her usual seat at a table off to the side of the dais, guiding her enchanted quill to transcribe every word that was said for the official record.

Tessa continued, addressing her eager audience. "We'll be allowing Delise and Maguire to gather their things, but they'll be escorted out of town this very night. Whosoever of you possess attack magic of any useful sort in this situation, please meet me up here immediately after the assembly is adjourned. We'd like to call on you to help me in overseeing their packing and leaving in case Delise gets any ambitious ideas."

"You got it!" a man yelled out from somewhere in the crowd.

Delise's mouth twitched at the corner, and I wondered if she might indeed be plotting some kind of, what?—escape made no sense. It was more likely she'd attempt some sort of final eff-you gesture. I hoped they didn't let her anywhere near the barrier spell. But of course she'd need to cross through it in order to exit the town.

It took me a while to realize Delise was laughing. Dark and menacing, the sound gave me the heebie-jeebies. I'd never liked the woman; it wasn't like there was much to like. But I'd never seen this side of her.

"How are you going to keep me out?" she asked the council. "The spell allows in anyone with magic. And you know I have more than most of you. Whenever I want to get back in, I will."

I tensed.

"Then we'll just have to adjust the spell to keep you out," Stella said, finally taking her seat again and crossing her arms over her chest.

"What, you'll adjust the spell like you did before, with Marla, the least powerful witch ever of all the Gawamas, bumbling around at the helm? Or do you forget that y'all barely managed to do it in the first place, and then once you did, I slipped my magic in there and no one even realized it? How would you even know if I came in again, or if I adjusted the magic to my suiting?"

Delise was oversimplifying things, and entirely leaving out the fact that I had noticed she was trying to modify the barrier spell. But I didn't have the chance to defend myself.

Nan lashed out like a barbed whip. "You talk trash about my granddaughter again and I'll yank out your tongue, wrap it around your head, and tie it up into a nice pretty bow that will match your hideous poncho thingy."

I was ninety-nine percent sure Nan would never do something like that.

Quade shot me a look, brows raised. I shrugged, grimacing. My grandmother kicked ass; his mom sucked. I didn't want to rub it in.

"Marla is a thousand times the woman you are," Nan went on. "And that's not just 'cause she's a Gawama, you hear. It's 'cause she's not afraid to own up to her mistakes on her way to becoming the best her. She's not afraid to care for others and to put herself out there in the process of helping Haveners, even if it means making a fool of herself, chasing after a nekked leprechaun draped in Spanx. She's our new detective, and she had a doozy of a first case."

My cheeks heated, but I had no idea if it was due to Nan's kind words, or due to the fact that everyone now knew I was the town's new detective and had spent the day chasing around Spanx and mischievous magical creatures. Nan could have instead mentioned how I'd solved a kidnapping—kind of— but nope. I got the Spanx and leprechaun. At least she hadn't mentioned him wagging around his privates in the sugar store.

"She even had to see the leprechaun's dangly bits, and she handled it like a champ."

Wincing, I felt my cheeks ramp up the temperature.

"Can you imagine that?" Nan continued in a loud, clear voice that carried all the way to the back, when all I wanted was for her to stop at this point. "Having to see a buck nekked little leprechaun's twig and berries? His sausage and meatballs? He got burned when Bab yanked him out of her sugar store, so he was probably waving his bits all around, trying to cool them."

"That he was," Bab yelled from the audience. "I ran into the back of my kitchen with Marla 'cause she told me he was there. Mind you, if not I might not've realized for a while, and he was headfirst in my sugar, bare butt mooning us like it was the middle of the damn night. I had to spend all afternoon scrubbing my kitchen to make sure it was clean again after him. But Marla solved the case and fixed what Delise did to the barrier, that's what Marla did. She saved the town."

Well, that wasn't exactly true, but I didn't have the chance to protest before the crowd began hooting and hollering their appreciation and even some congratulations.

Damn. Nan was doing a mighty fine job of sticking me with the role of detective. I didn't want it! Talking with snarky animals who were half insane was bad enough. Now I was going to have to don a Sherlock Holmes cap? Hair like mine didn't do hats.

"This is ridiculous," Delise called out, flapping her arms like wings under her poncho a few times, circling to face the audience of her peers. "Marla couldn't find her own ample ass with her own two hands! She ran away from town with her tail tucked between her legs because she was the runt of the family. She barely has any magic. She couldn't even make a marriage work. My son was always too good for her."

Whatever else Delise had been about to say about me, I wouldn't find out. Several things happened at once while I stood there in shock, unable to believe my eyes.

Quade stomped over to his mother while my

ninety-six-year-old nan rounded the table at mind-defying speeds and leapt down the foot or so that separated the dais from the floor of the main assembly hall. She landed on wobbly legs and almost crumpled, but my aunts were there to catch her.

As one, Nan, Aunt Jowelle, Aunt Luanne, and Aunt Shawna rounded on Delise.

"Quade," Nan growled, and he froze as he faced off with his mother.

Without turning around to look at them, he answered. "What?"

"I've always liked you. You always have my Marla girl's back even though this wretched woman is your mother. But this is for the Gawamas to handle."

Quade didn't move. The man who was gentle enough to coax plants to do his bidding shot molten anger at his mother—on my behalf.

My heart beat in my throat as I snapped back into myself, absorbing the fact that there was about to be a throwdown in my defense. I pushed off from the wall I'd been leaning against, planning to talk everyone down.

"Come on, Quade," Aunt Luanne said. "No one talks about our girl like that and gets away with it. Step back."

With evident regret, Quade did, but he hovered around the Gawama women as if planning to interfere once they did ... whatever they were going to do. My aunts and grandmother looked ready to claw Delise's eyes out, but my aunts were in their mid-to-late sixties, and Nan was nearing a hundred for sweet pickle's sake. Not one of them was a violent woman. Sure, they told you what they thought whether you asked them to or not, even if it was inappropriate and out of place, but they'd never brawled—as far as I knew.

My mouth open, ready to tell them all I didn't care what Delise said about me—even though I did at least a little—that's when Delise announced, loud enough for the whole hall to hear: "Marla Gawama is a stupid heifer. I don't see why you mind what I say about her. She's—"

Delise's eyes widened and she finally shut up.

I heard Noreen's enchanted pen scratch out the last of Delise's words into her large record of all town meetings. That was the one second of silence before the storm hit.

Aunt Shawna launched herself at Delise, knocking the woman flat onto her back with a sharp smack against the hardwood floor. The people sitting in the front pew, next to the spots my aunts had vacated, scrambled out of the way, as did Maguire, while Delise's mouth opened and closed, struggling for breath. When she finally did draw in breath, she wheezed through having the air knocked out of her lungs. Flat as a board, her feet stuck out from under Aunt Shawna like Delise was the Wicked Witch of the West. All she was missing were the striped socks and pointy shoes.

Aunt Shawna straddled Delise while Aunt Luanne tensed beside them like a beast about to attack.

"Take back what you said about Marla," Aunt Shawna ordered.

"No," Delise said. "Get off me, you cow."

Aunt Luanne crouched down next to them as Nan and Aunt Jowelle circled, looking for a way to help. Quade did the same, only I suspected he didn't intend to help in the same way my family did. He was probably looking to wrench the crazy women away from the crazy woman he was related to.

"Take it back," Aunt Luanne said, running her fingers obnoxiously across Delise's face.

Delise slapped Aunt Luanne's hands away. "No! You're about to throw me out. I'm not taking anything back."

Darnell Adams, Irma Lamont, Tessa Smate, and Stella Egerton descended the dais to surround us. I caught sight of people in the crowd flinging themselves from their seats and shuffling up the rapidly filling aisle to get a good view of the fight.

"You're not good enough to even speak Marla's name," Aunt Shawna said, though the statement was totally ridiculous. I wasn't some god or something. I was a divorcée with bad hair, a whole list of regrets I was trying not to have, and a doughnut addiction evidenced in my thighs.

"That's—" Delise started, but then Aunt Luanne all but put a finger up her nose. Delise whacked at my aunt's hand like it was a yellowjacket wasp ready to sting her.

"I think this has gone far enough," Darnell Adams said, adjusting his already straight bow tie despite the ludicrous show unfolding in front of him. "Is it the time of month for all of you when you go crazier than usual?"

With deadly slowness, Aunt Shawna swiveled atop her perch across Delise's waist to stare at Darnell. "Tell me you didn't just say what I think you said."

He *tsked*, frowning. "What kind of example are you setting for the youth in the assembly? Should they tackle a person just because they say something they don't like?"

"If that person is putting down someone they love, and the person won't shut the hell up," Aunt Luanne said, "even when they're warned to shut their trap, then hell yeah."

"That's immature," Darnell said, and then trailed off as Aunt Jowelle marched right up to him and lined herself up so she was staring straight into his eyes.

He cleared his throat, nervously adjusted his bow tie again, satin violet and green polka dots that day, and backed up half a step.

Go Aunt Jowelle. Where had all her rules about appropriate behavior gone? She was just as fierce in my defense as her sisters and mother.

But before the Gawamas could get going again, Tessa drew up to them.

"Punish her by banishing her from Gales Haven," she said. "That's the worst kind of punishment for someone with magic who doesn't know anything but what it's like to live in this town."

Aunt Shawna deliberated, trading a look with Aunt Luanne. "Fine," Shawna said before jumping off of Delise with the limberness of youth. Her regimen of multiple orgasms on the regular was obviously working to preserve her flexibility.

Before I could stop myself, and even though shit was dire, I glanced at Quade. His brow low and furrowed, he still looked gorgeous. His strength was apparent everywhere his muscles strained against his shirt and his jeans. The man was built, and what was even better, he was kind and gentle. He was more a man than Devin could ever dream of being. Seemed like it was time to begin my own multi-orgasmic workout regimen...

Nan snapped me out of my irrelevant thoughts. "Then close the assembly, Tessa. Let's throw her out on her butt now."

"You got it." Tessa climbed the step back onto the dais, spread her arms, and announced, "Show's over, everyone." Then she faced Noreen, who hadn't moved since chaos reigned, not one to abandon her post. "This assembly is now over. The council's verdict sentencing Delise and Maguire Contonn to banishment from the community of Gales Haven is final. This assembly is adjourned."

As voices rose and as many moved to exit as to go in the opposite direction to get a better view of Delise sprawled out on her ass, Tessa shouted, "Remember, anyone who can help guard the Contonns until we throw them out, please come up here."

People milled around me in all directions, making my head swim as the din grew louder and my family continued to voice its outrage.

Sinking to sit on the lip of the dais, I thought, *At least Clyde and Macy weren't here to see this.* They didn't need to witness their great-aunts and great-grandmother standing around glaring at Delise and cracking their knuckles like they were mobsters preparing for a beatdown.

And then I heard Clyde and Macy calling for me through the crowd.

CHAPTER TWENTY-TWO

CLYDE, Macy, and Harlow had arrived just in time to see both their families behaving like rabid baboons. Though I was secretly touched by Nan's and my aunts' defense of me, I didn't want my kids to think brawling was the answer to solving their problems. Macy's eyes brimmed with excitement as she recounted what Nan and her great-aunts had done. Clyde was the only one to have the grace to appear embarrassed, blushing intensely every time Macy again mentioned how Aunt Shawna leapt into the air and took Delise "right the hell down." Macy would smack her fist into her open palm for effect.

Each time Macy told the story, Aunt Shawna leapt higher and more gracefully. Already Macy was making her out to be a flipping gazelle, and the day was still young. Full-on hero worship was in effect for Aunt Luanne too—in fact, for all of my family who'd spoken their mind or gotten up in people's faces to defend my virtue. Macy had a girl crush on the Gawama women. I thought it was kind of cute that she admired the band of wild, redheaded women, of which I was most definitely a part.

Harlow, however, hadn't said much. When I finally asked her if she was all right, she shrugged and said it sucked to be Delise's granddaughter.

Yeah, it did. I thought it sucked to be Delise's anything, and set out to find the woman's disowned son when Clyde stopped me in my tracks.

"Where's Maguire?" he asked.

I whirled around looking for the man where I'd last seen him, next to his wife, then jumping out of the way to avoid my nutter family.

But Maguire's balding scalp was nowhere to be spotted, at least not among the mob that surrounded us. The crowd had thinned some, but most weren't eager to abandon the source of enough gossip to last through sparse times. Already I could picture the stories. Just as Macy's, they would stretch and exaggerate until the Gawama women were superheroes. Actually, Nan would probably get a kick out of it, so maybe it wasn't all bad.

"Hey!" I called out, though it wasn't easy to be heard above the din. "Does anyone see Maguire?"

The call was taken up and repeated until a confirmed response returned.

No one knew where Maguire was.

Tessa leaned into Delise, who was finally back on her feet, clutched on both sides by a large brawny and very hairy man I didn't recognize and a tiny, petite man who looked like a hard stare would break him in two. Even so, I had no doubt there was a very good reason why the petite man was on guard duty. There was one thing quickly learned in this community: outward appearances had little to do with one's power. If Tessa was entrusting Toothpick to guard one of the most important threats to Gales Haven since it was founded, then he packed a powerful punch behind his XS clothing.

Delise tried to pull her face back from Tessa, but the long-limbed blonde only pressed forward, further crowding her. "Where is Maguire?" Tessa barked.

"How should I know?" Delise snapped. "I've been dealing with wild beasts jumping on me, foaming at their big, fat mouths. So uncouth."

My three aunts, within hearing range, whirled on Delise and growled at the same time. My mouth dropped in surprise. It wasn't as much Aunt Shawna's reaction or Aunt Luanne's. Those women were passionate in everything they did. It was Aunt Jowelle who shocked me, and the fact that Nan appeared to be holding her back from Delise with a gnarled hand to her daughter's arm. Aunt Jowelle would never defy Nan, and especially not in public.

"Wait," Harlow said. "Where's my dad?"

"He probably helped my cowardly husband escape, leaving me behind," Delise said.

Aunt Jowelle feinted toward Delise, making her flinch. I didn't blame her this time. Aunt Jowelle looked ready to do some bitch slapping.

Harlow told her grandmother, "My dad would never do anything against this town, so that's not it."

"Then you don't really know your dad," Delise said, making me seethe inside. She was so incredibly unfit to be a mother, even of a grown man.

"Actually," Harlow said, "I do. I also know you."

Though Quade's sixteen-year-old daughter didn't say anything more, her meaning was implied. Standing there, surrounded by my children, her long chestnut hair framing her face, Harlow was a rock star, brimming with inner strength and integrity.

Delise had been outplayed. I saw the realization whisk across her face. She cringed before hurrying to erase the evidence of how she had been schooled by her granddaughter who was nothing like her.

"Does anyone see Quade?" Tessa called out.

When the consensus came back negative, my gut churned. I'd only just now found him again, I wasn't about to lose him.

My heart rate accelerated as I prepared to bash some heads in or scour the town, whatever it took to find him. No way was I going to do without him now that we were together again, our love quickly rekindling.

Clenching and unclenching my fists at my sides, I announced to no one in particular, "I'm going to find him," then marched up the aisle toward the double-door entrance.

"I'm coming with you." Harlow was right on my heels, my kids running up behind her.

I could see Nan up front, coordinating a search group when one of the side doors opened and in walked Quade and Maguire.

Relief rushed over me. I pivoted on my heel, swerved around my kids and his, and ran up the aisle.

Surprised, he turned just in time to catch me as I launched myself into his arms. Maguire hastily stepped away as I embraced his son.

"What's wrong?" Quade asked.

"I thought you were missing. We all did."

He shook his head with a smile softening his eyes. "I just wanted to have some time with my dad before he had to leave." He lowered his voice so only I could hear. "I needed some closure with him, to tell him how I felt about him."

I wasn't sure I wanted to know. I pitied Maguire,

not exactly a nice feeling, but one he'd been sparking in me since I first started dating his son and witnessed his parents' relationship.

Harlow drew up at our side, and Quade extended an arm to hug her without letting me go. Feeling like we were in an awkward, very public three-way hug with a family feel to it, I hastily beckoned my kids forward, pulling them into the huddle. There, that was better. I wasn't ready to think of what it would mean for our kids when Quade and I became an item again. At least they appeared to have become fast friends.

"Okay," Nan hollered, but her voice wasn't as strong as it'd been earlier, fueled by her ire.

Tessa took up the call. "Okay," she repeated. "Let's get Delise and Maguire packed and on their way."

Delise flinched as if she'd been struck. No one cared.

Maguire sagged all over.

"We're doing this without magic," Tessa said. "No zip-tripping. We don't want to risk any trouble. We're walking over to the Contonns' house."

When a team of bodyguards of all makes and sizes surrounded Tessa, they marched all together up the aisle, circling Delise and Maguire at their center. It wasn't lost on me that the wife and husband walked as far apart as they could within the confined space. It seemed Maguire had finally decided to take a stand against her now that it was too late. He'd have to wait for karma to run her over to return to the town.

"Should we go too?" I asked Nan once the group swept up the aisle and banged through the double doors into twilight.

"No," Nan answered. "They've got it handled. We have to figure out how we're going to keep Delise from trying to reenter the town, because she's right. The barrier spell is programmed to let her back in. So long as she still has magic, she'll be allowed inside the town."

"Why not block her the same way we added an exception for Macy?" I asked her. The rest of the council—minus Tessa—my aunts, Quade, and our kids surrounded us.

"Let's face it. We got lucky things worked out last time. If we can find another way, we have to do that first. We can't keep messing with the barrier spell and expect it to keep working. Humpty Dumpty can only be put back together so many times."

I didn't bother elucidating to my nan about Humpty Dumpty's true fate. Stories and facts became altered as they trickled from the outside world into our isolated town. The distortion wasn't unusual, it was the way of life here.

"I have an idea," a small voice announced. I

waited for everyone to react to it—until I noticed no one else did.

I started. "Oh, right. Only I can hear her."

All curious faces turned to me.

"Mindy. She said she has an idea." I bobbed my head this way and that. "But I don't see her."

"Do your eyes even work?" Mindy said, deprecating as usual. Fantastic. "Here I am. Walking along the pew in the very first row. Right up front. I don't see how you could miss me."

"Jeez. Back off with the smack, would you?" I snapped. "I couldn't see you. You're basically the size of a jellybean and a bunch of people are standing in front of you."

That's when I noticed everyone was watching me verbally spar with a hedgehog—and they could only hear what I said.

"Right," I mumbled. "Uh, so what's your idea?" I asked Mindy.

"Oh," she said. "So *now* you're finally paying attention to me, are you? Willing to hear what I have to say when you have no better ideas?"

"Yeah, that's right." My forced smile spread thin with impatience.

She waddled to the end of the front pew, opposite the aisle from where my aunts had been sitting, jumped to the floor, lost her balance, rolled into a tight ball, then popped open onto her feet again, almost without missing a beat. I had to admit, that was suave. In her place, I would've landed flat on my face, no doubt.

Like she was hundreds of times her size, she walked casually toward the middle of our haphazard gathering and stood still for a few moments before tilting her head upward and clearing her throat.

"Did she just ... clear her throat at us?" Darnell Adams asked.

I frowned. "She sure did. She has some attitude issues."

"So do you," Mindy said without giving up her regal posturing.

By then, most of the crowd had followed Delise and Maguire out, looking for more action. The hall had emptied except for a few stragglers, and those stragglers now walked toward us, scenting some more drama.

"Just get to the point," I told her, before once more remembering everyone was hearing me and not her. I didn't want to sound like a big bully when they couldn't tell my reactions were reasonable given how snarky the one-pound critter was.

"Fine," she said. "I'll organize the magical creatures of Gales Haven to form a guard to protect the barrier and keep Delise out until you can figure something better out."

Of course she'd been in the hall listening to

everything that was said. She'd warned me before that there was no place the magical creatures couldn't go. They had ears and eyes everywhere.

"Okay," I said. "I guess that would be good."

"You guess? Seriously? Like you have a better plan..."

Shit. We didn't. So instead of admitting to it, I relayed what she'd said.

"But," Mindy announced before anyone had a chance to respond, "I have three conditions."

I narrowed my eyes at her. "And what are those?"

"It will be your responsibility to deal with that leprechaun."

"Why is it mine?" I whined.

"Because you are the official detective of Gales Haven—"

"I am not."

She turned, rose onto her hind legs, and brought both front paws to what would be her waist in a human. Her meaning was oddly anthropomorphic, and also loud and clear.

Clyde chuckled, covering his mouth with his hand, and whispering out of the corner of his mouth at me in a sing-songy melody, "Oooh, you're in trouble."

"Knock it off," I told him, mostly because apparently I *was* in trouble. I didn't even know why.

"You are so the detective of Gales Haven," Mindy

said. "Your grandmother, the head of the council, said so."

Damn. Nan really had.

"Fine," I barked. "What are the other two conditions?"

"Hold up," she said, plopping back down onto all fours. "I wasn't finished. That leprechaun likes to cause all sorts of trouble."

"I know."

"It's entirely on you to keep him from causing problems for any of us creatures. We'll have enough on our plate protecting the town without watching out for that jackass."

"Oh-kay," I drew out.

"Wait," Darnell said. "Relay."

I sighed loudly. "She says she has three conditions for her and the other anima—I mean, creatures—defending the border until we figure out a better way to keep out Delise."

When I didn't continue—on purpose—Darnell prompted me.

"She basically says I have to continue being the detective of Gales Haven and deal with the leprechaun, whom she calls a jackass."

"That works," Nan said right away. "It's your job anyway."

"When exactly did it become my job?" I asked. "And don't I have a say in this?"

"Not really," Nan said with finality, not even answering all of my questions. "Keep going. Find out the other conditions. We could use their help. We'll post our guard too, but they can keep watch in a way we can't."

"Since when do we have a guard?" I asked.

"Since now."

"Oh, okay." Obviously. I pointed an impatient stare at the hedgehog, urging her to continue.

"Have you never heard the saying that you catch more bees with sugar than piss?"

"I'm pretty sure the saying doesn't go that way."

She shook her head, *tsking*. "I was just telling George how impossible you are to deal with."

"Excuse me?" My eyes bugged. "You're the one who's impossible!"

Quade touched my arm, and I sheepishly looked up at everyone observing my behavior.

I cleared my throat. "Will you please tell me your other two conditions?"

"Since you asked so nicely, of course." She smiled, the expression looking strangely at home on her little face amid a ring of quills. "Condition two is that you make some of your witches and wizards available to help any of us creatures if we need the assistance."

"What kind of help?"

"All sorts. Like right now Bob has a pricker stuck

in his butt and he won't stop whining about it." She held up her fingerless paws, waggling them. "None of us can get it out for him without putting our teeth on it, and no way are any of us putting our faces that close to the danger zone."

Grimacing, I asked, "Is it actually inside his butt?" Awkwardly, I looked around at the many watching faces. I lowered my voice, though it was useless. "Is it actually inside his ... butt hole?"

"What on earth are you talking about?" Aunt Jowelle asked, sounding alarmed and back to her usual disapproving self.

After relaying Mindy's request, the council agreed to this condition right away, thankfully making Bob's butthole no longer my business. I was apparently a detective, not an animal doctor.

"And the last condition?" I asked, steeling myself for what it might be.

Though Mindy spoke only to me, she turned and faced the council, tilting her head all the way back to mostly look up at them.

"I want to become the sixth member of the council. My kind needs representation, and I'm obviously the best suited for it. Besides, we creatures have been in Gales Haven as long as you all have been."

After I told the council members what Mindy wanted, they agreed to this final condition quickly.

"Really?" Mindy asked, breathless. "That's

wonderful news. I have to go share it with the creatures right now and start organizing us to defend our town from that ugly pink witch."

Then she waddled as quickly as she could back across the assembly hall before taking a sharp turn along the wall and disappearing. I had no idea how she was getting in and out since she obviously wasn't opening doors, but clearly she had her ways.

"What was that all about?" Stella asked.

I couldn't help a genuine smile. Mindy was a sparkplug, but her joy at this recognition she'd been wanting for so long for her and her people was cute. "She was really excited and wanted to go share the good news with the other critters."

"Ah," Stella said. "That's nice."

I nodded wistfully. It really was. Especially now that Mindy was gone and unable to give me crap.

Nan clapped her hands softly, reaching out for her daughters. Aunt Jowelle and Aunt Luanne scrambled to offer her the support she sought.

"That worked out well," Nan said. "We'd already decided to offer Mindy a seat on the council." Then she winked at me and allowed her daughters to lead her up the aisle like the queen she was.

CHAPTER TWENTY-THREE

DELISE and Maguire Contonn were escorted out of town late that night, when the moon was nearly full, looming large overhead, illuminating the sad scene. Much of the town turned out to see them off, and from what I hear, there was no gloating or goading of any kind. Everyone there was somber and respectful, realizing the full impact of what exile would mean to the couple who'd led a life of magic since their births. Delise and Maguire Contonn had been born and raised in this village, though Maguire had had a different surname until Delise ensnared him in her web. Neither one of them were equipped for a non-magical life. They'd have to learn how to do so many things all over again—without magic—and at their age I was sure it wasn't something they were looking forward to. Even a car loaded to the brim with their most precious belongings wouldn't be much help. They'd have to learn a new way of life.

It wasn't even the lack of magic that would be the worst part. They'd given up the support of a tight-knit community. Despite personal preferences and the odd assortment of discordant personalities, Haveners had each other's backs—no matter what. When times got tough, you could count on having thousands of people behind you, helping you get through whatever the challenge was.

I'd never been more grateful that I finally decided to return home. I could kick my earlier self in the behind for being so foolish and not properly valuing this kind of support.

At least I was here now. At least my kids would experience Gales Haven while there was still time for them to adjust and become a part of this world. With how accepting of magic they were, I had no doubt they'd adapt in no time.

I'd offered Quade my company in seeing his parents off, but he must have noticed my exhaustion. It had been a very long last few days, during which far too much had gone wrong—and so much had ended up right. Like a gentleman, he'd declined, assuring me he'd be fine and had all the support he needed. Harlow was at his side, and Clyde and Macy were going too, with Nan and my aunts. I was the only one who didn't want to go see the show, or to make sure the Contonns actually made it across the border and didn't immediately try to turn back.

The council didn't even trust them to drive their own car across the barrier, though I'm not sure what they feared. That Delise would point the vehicle at the crowd and try to take down as many people with her as she could, like a sick game of bowling, where the people were the pins? Maybe. I wouldn't put it past her. Somewhere along the way, Delise had allowed herself to become a dark, spiteful person. The town would be better off without her.

So would Quade.

One of the guards had driven their car across the barrier, pointed it away from here, and left it idling. The Contonns' exile was official and final.

Once I was convinced that Quade genuinely didn't need me there at his side, I remained home all on my own, indulging in the moments of quiet and his guilt-free pass. I craved stillness like I craved Bab's pastries, and I relished in its unexpected arrival. Even when I'd been married to Devin, I'd been largely alone. I hadn't had a true partner, someone to lean on. And kids didn't count. I loved mine to pieces, but they always needed something or other, and the need to constantly be present for them —even when they weren't physically with me—was real and draining.

I'd learned to rely on me-time to replenish. In

Gawama Mama House, the quiet moments would be far and few between. Especially since I had plans to jump Quade at the earliest opportunity and then continue making up for lost time.

I sat by myself on the back porch, taking in the way the back yard, which was more of a nature preserve than any kind of yard, pulsated seemingly in tune with my slow breaths. Large oaks rose up from the ground in great thick, twisted trunks, their leaves hanging low, swaying and sweeping in a mesmerizing crackle that reminded me of both the rain and the ocean at once, effectively whisking away every concern. The little warm white lights that Grandpa Oscar had set around the wild garden for me when I was a girl continued to blink and hover like they were fireflies instead of a long-lasting spell that survived my grandpa's death. The long grass shushed and oscillated like it was rocking to soothe an infant.

I drew great comfort from the familiar scene, allowing it to flow through me and smooth any rough edges. To replenish me where I was depleted.

Things might not be perfect, but they were well enough.

Rocking gently in a rocking chair that Great-Great-Granny Jemima's own father had built, and had been since preserved by every subsequent generation of Gawamas, the creaking set the beat of the night like a metronome.

My kids had been too excited by all the happenings in town to slow down much before they left. Macy had recounted the story of how Aunt Shawna had "kicked Delise's nasty ass" approximately three hundred times until she finally tired of it. Even so, I'd managed to slip a quick question in about how their first day of school went.

As usual, their responses were largely unhelpful. "Great" and "awesome" weren't exactly highly descriptive, but they were promising. In the non-magical world, when they'd attended an average public high school, their responses had ranged from "it sucked" to "it was okay." I was taking the upgrade as a good sign. I'd grill them for elaboration later. For now, they were happy, which made me happy—and incredibly relieved.

I'd taken a big risk bringing them here, but it was as clear as Great-Great-Granny Jemima's crystal ball —which resided permanently in the parlor—that it was working out. The barrier spell was repaired. Macy was safe to remain within it. Both my kids had magic in spades and were beginning to manifest in a place where they'd be guided along to their fullest potential—and hopefully would no longer be at risk of blowing up the place.

Delise and Maguire were gone. A guard

composed of witches, wizards, and creatures was already in place, making sure they couldn't return until a better system was discovered and instituted.

I hadn't seen any more signs of the wily leprechaun, nor had I heard anything more from Jadine Lolly, who apparently had been consumed in her passion for Jelly Frumpers. The rumors were already circling town even while there were more pressing matters at hand. No doubt, within days the whirlwind affair between Jadine and Jelly would become a favorite topic of gossip.

There was no accounting for taste, but hopefully Jelly's appreciation would bolster Jadine's confidence and her obsession with Spanx would pass. If I never heard the word *Spanx* again in my life, I'd do a dance in celebration.

I still hadn't had the time to catch up with Wanda, nor to discover what was in her secret back room that my sexed-up aunts loved, but there'd be time for that. Without having to chase a *nekked* leprechaun, there'd be time for lots of activities I was ready to once more enjoy.

There was still the teeny tiny issue of me being some sort of magical sponge or buffer, depending on whether you asked Leonie or Harlow, but the fact hadn't interfered with my life, so I was hoping it would just fade away. I had enough to handle with my own abilities and the host of snarky magical creatures who wanted to chat with me without borrowing power from others. I was just fine without it. The whole sponge slash buffer situation could just float on by and leave me be, thanks very much.

There was also the issue of my new work detail. Never in my life had I pictured myself being a detective—of any sort. Half the time I couldn't find my sunglasses when they rested on my own head. The chances of me becoming some awesome Sherlylock Holmes were slim to none, so now that the crisis with the barrier spell was fully over, I planned to talk some sense into my nan.

No one was going to want me running all over town bungling every case I got. They needed me to interpret for all the critters within Gales Haven's borders? Fine. I'd learn to live with that. Maybe Mindy and I would eventually even become friends. Perhaps she'd stop insulting me, and George would come to think me brilliant. I might even learn to tolerate Humphrey. Why not? I was feeling generous. So much had gone right that I could learn to forgive him for interrupting my one chance at some serious shmexy time in recent memory.

Crickets erupted into a chorus of chirps, contributing to the idyllic night. A subtle breeze drifted across the Gawama land, turning up the volume on the rustling of the leaves and the swaying of the grasses. I could stay out here all night, and I fully planned to until the family returned from seeing the exiles off and smothered my quiet with their usual loud and chaotic natures.

I took a long pull from my bottle of Beebee's brew. I hadn't yet had the chance to stop by Beebee's Beer Bar or Mabel's Medicinal and Restorative Herbs for Healing and Relaxation shop, though both stops were high on my list. Right up there with visiting Mo Ellen for an eat-whatever-I-want spell.

Condensation dripping down my hand, I clutched one of Aunt Luanne's bottles. The glass of the bottle was mellow yellow with a label pronouncing this particular brew *Take a Chill Pill*, so I figured it'd be just right. I planned to do a whole lot of chilling now that I was doing some serious hoping that my leprechaun problems were finally over. How much trouble could one leprechaun cause magical creatures anyway? He might have just moved on from town, figuring it wasn't worth the trouble of having me chase him all over the place.

My next day: help the kids to the bus stop and then go for a nice, relaxing run. Shower, then one of Aunt Jowelle's awesome breakfasts. Next, stop by Bab's to cheat on Aunt Jowelle with some Enchanted Hearts, and buy Twisted Turtles for later. I'd check in on Quade and Wanda, then go get the spell started with Mo Ellen.

"Mind sharing?" a squeaky voice asked.

My free hand jerked to my chest and I jostled my beer, sloshing some on my unicorn-and-rainbow print leggings. They were purple, sparkly, and come on ... unicorns and rainbows. They were so dorky that they crossed the line into super cool zone—no matter what my kids said to the contrary—and they were some of my favorites, especially since they concealed the cellulite in my butt and thighs like a champ.

"Humphrey," I bit out. "You just made me spill!"

"I didn't make you do anything. It's not my fault you're as skittish as my second cousin Petunia. She'll jump at anything at all. She does no favors to our reputation as fierce creatures."

"Your reputation isn't fierce. The saying goes, 'As skittish as a mouse.'"

"No way. You've got it all wrong. That makes no sense. I'm not skittish in the least."

"You also aren't a normal mouse."

Humphrey scampered across the porch in the moonlight before standing up, puffing out his little chest. "Granted. I'm special. Brilliant and sharp-minded."

"You're a very annoying mouse, that's what you are. With horrible timing."

He gasped, a tiny paw traveling to his chest in affront before he lowered back down to all fours. "I am *not* annoying. And my timing is impeccable.

Also, don't forget to call me Hugh. That's my name."

"That is not your name, *Humphrey*. You were going to watch Quade and I have sex like a total perv! I didn't even know you were there."

"Well, yeah, that was kind of the point. I didn't want you to stop. I just wanted to watch. And it's Hugh."

"Humphrey," I said, dragging out every syllable until the mouse growled. "That's not right. Don't you know that? Having sex is a private affair. No one's supposed to watch."

He sat on his haunches and scratched at his chin. "Are you sure?" he asked. "And it's *Hugh*. I'm cool Hugh."

"I'm totally sure," I said. Of course I was. Duh. Or better yet, *fuh*. "People are supposed to have sex in private without anybody watching."

He looked at me, tiny forehead furrowed. "Do your Aunt Luanne and Aunt Shawna know that? Because I saw them—"

"Humphrey."

"I won't respond to that."

"Fine. Hugh," I grumbled. "I don't want to hear about my aunts' sex lives. Not now, not ever. Got it?"

"All right ... I guess. But it's your loss. What they get up to is highly entertaining. Whenever they go out on their dates, I try to make sure I'm in the right place to—"

"Humphrey, I'm not kidding," I said. "You've already possibly ruined my favorite pants. I don't want you souring my mood too. No one needs to picture their aunts doing ... that stuff."

He shrugged, tiny shoulders moving. "Like I said, your loss. And call me Humphrey one more time and I'll make sure I'm positioned to watch every time you try to get it on. Maybe I'll even bring friends. Petunia isn't skittish about watching good action. Neither is Basil. He's so stupid we tell him you guys are tickling each other and he buys it."

"That's terrible!"

Humphrey shrugged again, whiskers twitching in indifference. Then he pointed his attention at my legs and silver-sequined Converse. Defensively, I drew my legs up and tucked my feet partially under my crossed thighs.

"You like those leggings?" he asked.

"Yeahhhh. I love them."

"Are they your kids'?"

"No, they're mine."

"Oh." He frowned. "I thought that might explain it. Have you actually looked at them?"

"Humphr—"

He narrowed his eyes at me and I was *not* going to call his bluff on this one. No way did I want a repeat of finding Humphrey munching on popcorn above me.

"*Hugh*, will you please just go away?"

"Man, I just got here."

"You can give me grief another time, okay? Or even better, you can just not. But I need some downtime before everyone shows back up."

"You mean you like being alone?"

I nodded. "Definitely. I love it."

"I came over because I felt bad for you, all alone like this. I don't like being alone. I was coming to keep you company."

"Aw, Hugh. That's actually pretty sweet of you, even if it was misguided."

"Shh!" The mouse whipped his head around in every direction before settling back on me. "Don't call me that. I have a reputation to preserve. There are ears everywhere, especially when you can't see anybody."

"I'll keep that in mind," I said with a raised brow.

"You be sure to do that. Or else I won't come visit you again."

"Is that a promise?"

"It is."

"Hmm." I smiled, and I didn't think Humphrey was getting it. "Maybe it'd be better if you go tonight. So I don't risk tarnishing your hardened reputation."

"Probably wise." He twitched his whiskers

around a serious scowl. "There's only so much damage I can recover from."

Without another word, he skittered away, disappearing into the shadows along the corner of the porch, probably squeezing through a small hole no one noticed.

Sighing loudly, I leaned back into my rocker, preparing to put Humphrey clear out of my mind and make the most of whatever time I had left before the Gawamas returned. I took a long sip of *Take a Chill Pill*, loving the taste of it. It was like mint chocolate chip ice cream rolled around in sprinkles. Smacking my lips, I dragged the rocking chair closer to the railing and sat back down, kicking my legs up onto it, crossing them at the ankles, and experiencing a deep sense of contentment.

The night was a bit chilly, but pleasant enough. I drank some more brew ... and froze.

"Motherfreaking little freak," I growled, shooting to my feet.

The leprechaun streaked by—maybe twenty feet in front of me—still wearing nothing but Spanx, meaning I'd gotten a clear view of those bubbly butt cheeks and proof that leprechauns were hung just like the males of most other species. His orange hair was dark as blood beneath the pale moonlight as he ran for all he was worth. He disappeared behind large, gnarled roots within seconds.

Just as a whole family of raccoons, looking like masked bandits in the night, tore after him.

"Wha...?" I muttered. "What the hell did he do to piss them off like that?"

I watched as a half dozen raccoons disappeared into the long shadows the trees cast, no doubt still fast on the leprechaun's trail.

For a whole thirty seconds, I deliberated chasing after them. I was kind of supposed to catch that blasted leprechaun—at least until I convinced Nan to give me another job that suited me better. Taste tester for Bab's Bopping Boopy Bakery or Three-Hundred-Sixty-Nine Fabulous Feisty Flavors? I'm your woman. On a bold day, I'd even be a tester for the mysterious back room of Wanda's Cock, Coffee, and Cocoa Café, which was daring given it was one of Aunt Luanne's and Aunt Shawna's favorite haunts.

The mewling of raccoons, possibly even the leprechaun, filtered across the otherwise peaceful field, suggesting a scuffle of some sort. No doubt the leprechaun had done something to deserve his punishment.

I took another sip of my brew, then made my decision.

Sinking back down into the rocker, I got comfortable, kicking my sneaks off before I crossed my feet up on the railing. I settled in.

For tonight, I wasn't taking on any problems.

They could wait. At this rate, the leprechaun would still be in town causing trouble tomorrow.

I smiled out into the moonlit night that crawled with magical creatures and dense magic. I was in my element.

Rocking back and forth a few times, I allowed the peace of knowing I was exactly where I was supposed to be to settle over me. Like a mantle, it kept me warm and looking forward to the future— no matter how many crazy cases it might include.

Regardless, tomorrow would be a bright dawn.

CHARMED CAPER

Witches of Gales Haven - **Book Three**

Continue the wild adventures with Marla and the rest of the Gawamas in *Charmed Caper*!

BOOKS BY LUCÍA ASHTA

~ FANTASY BOOKS ~

WITCHING WORLD UNIVERSE

Witches of Gales Haven
Perfect Pending
Magical Mayhem
Charmed Caper

Magical Creatures Academy
Night Shifter
Lion Shifter
Mage Shifter
Power Streak
Power Pendant
Power Shifter

Sirangel

Siren Magic

Angel Magic

Fusion Magic

Magical Arts Academy

First Spell

Winged Pursuit

Unexpected Agents

Improbable Ally

Questionable Rescue

Sorcerers' Web

Ghostly Return

Transformations

Castle's Curse

Spirited Escape

Dragon's Fury

Magic Ignites

Powers Unleashed

Witching World

Magic Awakens

The Five-Petal Knot

The Merqueen

The Ginger Cat

The Scarlet Dragon

Spirit of the Spell

Mermagic

Light Warriors

Beyond Sedona

Beyond Prophecy

Beyond Amber

Beyond Arnaka

PLANET ORIGINS UNIVERSE

Dragon Force

Invisible Born

Invisible Bound

Invisible Rider

Planet Origins

Planet Origins

Original Elements

Holographic Princess

Purple Worlds

Mowab Rider

Planet Sand

Holographic Convergence

OTHER WORLDS

Supernatural Bounty Hunter

(co-authored with Leia Stone)

Magic Bite

Magic Sight

Magic Touch

Pocket Portals
The Orphan Son

STANDALONES

Huntress of the Unseen
A Betrayal of Time
Whispers of Pachamama
Daughter of the Wind
The Unkillable Killer
Immortalium

~ ROMANCE BOOKS ~

Seize Your Wild
Dream Gone Wild

ACKNOWLEDGMENTS

I'd write no matter what, because telling stories is a passion, but the following people make creating worlds (and life) a joy. I'm eternally grateful for the support of my beloved, James, my mother, Elsa, and my three daughters, Catia, Sonia, and Nadia. They've always believed in me, even before I published a single word. They help me see the magic in the world around me, and more importantly, within.

I'm thankful for every single one of you who've reached out to tell me that one of my stories touched you in one way or another, made you laugh or cry, or kept you up long past your bedtime. You've given me reason to keep writing.

And a special thank you to the members of my reader group, AKA my magical creatures. Your constant enthusiasm and love for my books makes me want to write all the more, and I already geek out over writing. These stories are for you.

ABOUT THE AUTHOR

Lucía Ashta is the Amazon top 100 bestselling author of young adult, new adult, and adult paranormal and urban fantasy books, including the series *Magical Creatures Academy*, *Witches of Gales Haven*, *Sirangel*, *Magical Arts Academy*, *Witching World*, *Dragon Force*, and *Supernatural Bounty Hunter*.

When Lucía isn't writing, she's reading, painting, or adventuring. Magical fantasy is her favorite, but the romance, laughs, and quirky characters are what keep her hooked on books.

A former attorney and architect, she's an Argentinian-American author who lives in Sedona with her beloved and three daughters. She published her first story (about an unusual Cockatoo) at the age of eight, and she's been at it ever since.

Sign up for Lucía's newsletter:
https://www.subscribepage.com/luciaashta

Connect with her online:
LuciaAshta.com
AuthorLuciaAshta@gmail.com

Hang out with her:
https://www.facebook.com/groups/LuciaAshta

facebook.com/authorluciaashta

bookbub.com/authors/lucia-ashta

amazon.com/author/luciaashta

instagram.com/luciaashta

Made in the USA
Columbia, SC
08 November 2021

48524547R00205